The Curse
of Hannah's Gate

The Curse
of Hannah's Gate

Daoma Winston

Thorndike Press • Chivers Press
Thorndike, Maine USA   Bath, Avon, England

This Large Print edition is published by Thorndike Press, USA and by Chivers Press, England.

Published in 1995 in the U.S. by arrangement with Jay Garon Brooke Associates, Inc.

Published in 1995 in the U.K. by arrangement with Piatkus Books, Ltd.

U.S.   Hardcover   0-7862-0218-1 (Romance Series Edition)
U.K.   Hardcover   0-7451-3098-4 (Chivers Large Print)
U.K.   Softcover   0-7451-3099-2 (Camden Large Print)

The text of this Large Print edition is unabridged.
Other aspects of the book may vary from the original edition.

Set in 16 pt. News Plantin by Juanita Macdonald.

Printed in the United States on permanent paper.

British Library Cataloguing in Publication Data available

Library of Congress Cataloging in Publication Data

Winston, Daoma, 1922–
       The curse of Hannah's gate / Daoma Winston.
          p.   cm.
       ISBN 0-7862-0218-1 (lg. print : hc)
       1. Large type books.   I. Title.
    [PS3545.I7612C87   1995]
    813'.54—dc20   94-37508

For Murray
Who still makes all things possible

Chapter One

It was just before Christmas. Vari-coloured lights glistened in shrubbery along the way, and twinkled in the huge old magnolia trees that flanked the house known as Hannah's Gate.

This part of the city of Washington, located just west of Connecticut Avenue, was called Cleveland Park, after President Grover Cleveland, who had once owned a country cottage there.

It was a place of many streams channelled into culverts, and hills and ravines, and was famous for aged trees — oak, dogwood, bamboo, mimosa and honey locust — for which this road, Honey Locust Lane was named.

Elianne Merrill walked slowly up its narrow curving length, remembering how the trees looked in the spring when they were foamy with white blossoms. It was three years since she had seen them that way. The last time she had looked up at them their limbs had been bare and black against the sky. As bare and black as they were right now.

She was a tall girl, very thin, her cheeks hollowed, her eyes dark and shadowed. Her hair was auburn, and fell to her waist in a thick cascade of curls and waves. She wore faded grey jeans, torn at one pocket, and a lightweight jacket. Her sneakers were too large, and clumsy on her sockless feet. From a distance, she looked like a very young child. But seen close up, she seemed much older than her eighteen years. There was sorrow in her eyes, and pain. There was dread too.

Now, straightening her shoulders, easing the straps of the backpack she carried, she paused before the polished brass sign that said 'Hannah's Gate'.

It was a big old Victorian house, built in the 1890s. There were three storeys, including an attic room for servants. A huge front porch ran across the front.

Elianne had seen pictures of it when its paint was peeling, and its curlicued wooden trim was splintered. Now it was a luxurious dwelling, cared for and beautiful. Still, when she had lived there, it was a place of shadows, of secrets, of whispers in the night. Was it the same? she wondered. Or had it finally changed?

Through most of her growing-up years

there, her father, Leigh Merrill, had devoted himself to restoring the house to what it had been in her great grandfather's time. He, Big Jack Gowan, once a senator from Mississippi, had built Hannah's Gate, and named it that after her great-grandmother.

It was Elianne's father, though, who had changed it from a house into an estate that covered a huge square block enclosed within tall red brick walls.

Elianne had fled those walls in anguish and rage. Now she had come home again.

She shivered suddenly. With cold, but also with fear. She wondered what her father would say, and what she would reply.

She had come so far. But now that she was here, uncertainty grew in her. Unconsciously her hands went to her hair, stroking, smoothing. It was as if she were reassuring herself that the long silken strands were real. Sometimes, she still felt the ice-cold blade of the scissors pressing against her scalp as her father had cut the long tresses away and thrown them to the floor.

She had lived through those moments so many times in her thoughts. She didn't want to, but now she lived through them once again.

It had been early January of 1968. She'd been alone in the house, playing a Bob Dylan record.

Her father had banged on her bedroom door, yelled, 'Elianne, stop that crap!'

She stopped the music at once, but he hadn't gone away. He'd banged on the door again. 'I want to talk to you.' When she opened the door, he said, 'My God, you look like a bum. I won't have it in my house. As long as you live here, you'll do as I say.'

She glared at him. She couldn't help it. What did he want? Why couldn't he leave her alone? First it was the music. Now it was how she looked. In a minute it would be something else. He was so unfair. Unfair . . .

Her silence made him even more angry. 'Get a hair cut,' he said. 'I want you to look like a lady.'

She had protested that she didn't want to. She liked her hair long as it was. All the girls wore it that way. She didn't want to be different.

But he found shears in his room, thrust them at her, told her to use them, then and there, as he stood watching. When she refused, he forced her down on the edge of the bed. Quickly, he hacked away great clumps of her hair, allowing them to fall from his fingers like auburn rain.

When he stopped, her head was shorn except for a two-inch brush through which patches of scalp shone. He let her go, and she sagged, weeping, to the pillows.

Late that night, having cried until she could cry no longer, she had known what she would do. She couldn't live like a caged bird forever. There was freedom somewhere, and she was going to it. At dawn, she had silently closed the iron gate in the wall around Hannah's Gate, and had walked down Honey Locust Lane.

Now, looking up at the house, she thought that soon she would be singed once again by the flame of her father's hatred. But maybe it would be different after all this time. Maybe, in her absence, he would have discovered for her a father's love.

At last, hesitantly, she went through the gate, past the magnolia trees. She climbed the steps and knocked at the door.

Immediately there were quick recognizable footsteps. Her mother!

The door flew open. Elianne looked into familiar brown eyes, into a well-known and joyful face.

'Elianne! Oh, my dear,' Claire Merrill said.

It was the first time in years that Elianne had heard her name said aloud. She discovered that she liked the sound of it.

'Oh, my dear girl, I've waited so long! I'm so happy to see you,' her mother said, holding her tightly. 'Come in. Come in. Thank God, you're home.'

But Elianne, on the threshold, hesitated once again. She was waiting to see her father. Would he accept her? Would they be able to begin anew as father and daughter? She had never cut her hair since the terrible day he had cut it himself. It was long ago, but that meant little. She knew she was different now, in her looks and her manner. Would he notice?

But he didn't appear. No one else did. Neither her Grandma Dora, nor her two brothers.

She allowed her mother to draw her into the foyer. It seemed the same to her. The huge cutglass chandelier hanging overhead . . . the mahogany table . . . the curved oak bannister . . . She didn't notice the huge vase of carnations near the door, nor the motor-driven cage made of gilt bars and glass walls that was the new lift only recently installed beside the staircase. Although the room was bright, it seemed to her that she saw lingering shadows there, and heard echoes of whispered conversations.

She knew that coming home held many dangers. She didn't know what they would be, or where they would come from. Her father? Yes. But she would try to deal with that possibility when it arose. Her brothers? Again, she would try. But they had been her enemies once, although she never understood why. She remembered her beloved doll that her Uncle

Brett, on a visit from Boston, had given her. Decapitated. Arms and legs torn off. At the foot of her bed, propped on cushions. When Elianne had touched her, the doll had fallen apart, and she had recalled how, earlier that morning, she had heard her older brother Gordon's whisper and her brother David's giggle. But, of course, they had only been children then.

Claire Merrill held her daughter for another long moment. She felt the shivering of her slight body. But, still smiling, her joyful eyes misty, she said, 'We must talk, Elianne. There are things I must tell you.'

Claire was a young-looking forty-nine. Her hair was deep auburn, with only a few silver strands. It was drawn back from her heart-shaped face in a smooth French twist. Her skin was unlined, the dimples of her childhood remaining beside her mouth. She was trim, with very good legs. Her eyes were dark brown and expressive, always reflecting her feelings.

Now the joy was gone from them. They became sombre. She was thinking ahead to what she must say. She had known these first few moments would be hard, but faced with them, she found herself struggling for composure. She must tell Elianne quickly, as carefully as she could. She had planned for this ever since her daughter had telephoned early in the past October, saying, with heart-wrenching uncertainty, 'Mama, can I come home? Is it all right? Oh, Mama, I need so to come home.'

Now, looking into Elianne's eyes, glad that they were alone in the house, she drew the young girl with her, through the foyer, and into the study close by.

Elianne gazed at the room. It was the same as always. The portrait of her great grandfather, Big Jack Gowan, still hung on the wall, ruddy-faced, faintly smiling. His hair was frosted with white, but showed auburn streaks the same shade as Claire's, the same very nearly as Elianne's own. He looked powerful and important, just as her Grandma Dora had always spoken of him. But, of course, Elianne had never known him. He'd died long before she was born.

The rest of the study too was as she remembered. She sank into the big chair, first dropping her backpack beside it. This one had been her father's favourite. Its softness enwrapped her briefly. She realized that she was very tired, very hungry too. But neither seemed important. She leaned forward, asking, because she could wait no longer, 'Where is everybody? Grandma Dora? The boys? And Dad? Where's Dad?'

Claire seated herself on the chair arm. She took Elianne's hand. It was cold to her touch, thin as an autumn leaf. She said gently, 'Elianne, your grandmother died. It was just a week after you called.' Claire paused briefly, remembering how it had been. Her nephew, Keith, worried that Dora hadn't come down to breakfast, had been waiting when Claire walked down the steps. She herself, becoming concerned, had hurried up to her mother's room. She had gone in. First she'd believed that her mother was asleep. But then, realizing the absoluteness of the silence, she had bent close to her mother, and understood that she was dead. Claire went on: 'She had no illness. No pain. No period of suffering or fear. It happened as she slept. But, oh, my darling, she was so happy the last few days. Because she had spoken to you, and knew you were coming home.'

'I wish she had waited for me.' Elianne said, her voice shaking. 'I wish I could have come home sooner.'

'So do I. But that was not to be.' Once again Claire paused. Now she had to say the most hurtful words of all. She had to do it quickly. She said, 'There's more, Elianne. About your father.'

'About Dad? What do you mean? What's wrong?'

'It happened a few months after you left. It was in April. The day that Martin Luther King was killed. That night . . . that night your father became ill. He died very soon afterwards.'

Claire had decided long before that the barest of details were enough. Elianne had no need to know more. So she said nothing of the telephone call that had brought her to the sleazy hotel, driving through the still smoking city . . . nothing of the ride to the hospital . . . and nothing of that one final drinking binge that had ended Leigh Merrill's life.

Elianne, her eyes wide with disbelief, whispered, 'Dad? He's dead? You mean that I'm too late after all. You mean that now I'll never know why he hated me?'

'He didn't hate you. It was something in himself that he hated. You must believe me, and try to understand. It was never you. There was the war . . . and after he came back . . . Oh, if only you'd known him before . . .'

'Before . . .' she whispered. The *before* didn't matter to Elianne. What mattered was that he was gone. Whatever had been wrong between them now couldn't be undone.

Claire waited a moment. She saw the pain deepen in Elianne's eyes and said gently, 'He loved you. He loved both of us. Somehow,

16

because of whatever it was that happened to him, he couldn't show it.' The lie came easily to Claire's lips. It was for her child's sake. For Elianne, she could tell that lie. But Claire herself knew the truth. From the instant that Leigh had known that his first child was a girl, he had resented her. He had resented her until the day he died. And all that time, for all those fifteen years, he'd blamed Claire for having had a daughter, and continued to blame her even after she'd given him two sons.

Elianne, clasping her hands tightly in her lap, told herself that the past couldn't be changed. It was done. Over. Nothing could be done about it. She had learned that lesson well in the years she'd been gone.

Now Claire said, 'And there's something else I must tell you. It's about me. I . . . I was alone for three years, Elianne. It was very hard. Although I mightn't seem so to you, I'm still quite a young woman. I'd been lonely for such a long time. I met someone. First at Anna Taylor's house — you do remember her, don't you? And then again, in London. A month ago he came here, and we've married. His title is Lord Creighton. His real name is Ollie Duvaney. He's a fine man and very good to me. I know that you'll like him. He'll be home later this evening. Your brothers will be home soon, I think.' Then, drawing a quick breath, she went on, 'Oh, Elianne, I tried so hard to find you. Where did you go? What did you do? How did you live?'

'Where did I go?' Elianne repeated vaguely. 'What did I do?' She looked into her mother's face. There was such a lot to say, to explain. It was too hard. She couldn't do it now. 'There'll be time later to talk about it, Mama.'

'Yes,' Claire agreed. 'There'll be time.'

From outside came the sound of a car in the driveway. Voices that were still familiar to her: Gordon and David.

She stiffened, preparing herself.

Gordon came into the study first. He was nearly sixteen and had reached his full growth, almost as tall as his father had been, but clumsy on his feet, and very robust. He had thick upper arms and a heavy chest. His cheeks were full, making his dark eyes seem narrow slits.

He stopped short on the threshold, staring at Elianne, mouth drawn tight. Finally he said, 'Mom told me you'd be coming back. I didn't really believe you would.' He paused. Then: 'I guess all I can say is, "Welcome home, Elianne." '

His tone was pleasant enough. The words were acceptable. Yet neither rang true. Elianne sensed that what he said had nothing to do with what he was thinking.

David was tall now too, but unlike Gordon looked very similar to his father. He had the same long hazel eyes, the same narrow rangy build. He was about fourteen, but there was something old in his expression. He said cautiously, 'It's been a long time, hasn't it?'

She remembered how often Gordon had whispered secretly to David. She wondered if he still did.

Later she remembered those moments as the hardest part of her homecoming. More difficult even than learning that her father had died, and her Grandma Dora. More difficult because it was then that she learned that, although her brothers had better manners than when they were children, their feelings were unchanged.

But now, as they spoke, she wondered what would happen if they knew the truth about her life in her years away. If they had seen her in the grip of Jake Babbitt's beliefs, when she accepted them and him, when she thought she loved him. . . .

Jake . . . her mind was full of him as her mother took her up to her old room, and left her to wash and change and rest for a little while.

Jake . . . She looked past the leafless tendrils of the wistaria vine that covered part of the window, along with a good bit of the back of the house. She looked past it, down the long slope to the swimming pool and the cottage beside it. She didn't notice when lights suddenly brightened its windows.

She was remembering the first time she saw Jake.

She was in a Missouri diner, drinking coffee she didn't know how she would pay for. Some kind of a policeman, wearing a star on his brown leather jacket, a big hat, and high boots, was staring hard at her. She tried to tell herself it didn't mean anything. Wherever she was people seemed to give her that kind of look. She supposed it was her clothes, the cap she wore to cover her awful hair. She supposed it was because she was alone. But why? They must be used to people travelling alone. There were plenty of kids on the road now. She had seen, even linked up with briefly, any number of them. She slid another look at the policeman. He was still staring at her.

She'd come this far hitching rides from truck drivers. She'd hoped to go on, further west, the same way. But she couldn't sit here, wait to get a ride, not with him staring at her.

She tried to slip away, but he followed her outside. He stopped her and asked, 'Where you going, girl?'

Rain and wind burned her cheeks. His fingers clenched into her arm, burned her flesh.

A dark van pulled in, sweeping both of them with its headlights. A door slammed. A man, big, stooped and bearded, peered at them from beneath a wide-brimmed black hat.

The policeman grimaced in disgust. 'A whole tribe of you freaks coming through.'

The man went inside. But within moments he was back, saying, 'The girl's coffee is paid for now. The diner's owner told me she doesn't want any trouble.' His voice was slow and deep. Dark eyes shone out of the grooved shadows of his face. White teeth glimmered in the forest of his beard.

'And how come you're butting in?'

'I heard the lady belly-aching about getting cheated on the coffee. I paid for it. She told me she didn't want any trouble,' the man answered.

The policeman spat, turned away. 'Get your asses out of this town, hear me!'

The bearded man, Jake Babbitt, said, 'Come on. I'll give you a ride.' He boosted Elianne up to the front seat of the van, and pulled out quickly.

'Thank you,' she said. 'I don't know what would have happened if you hadn't turned up.'

'It was meant to be,' he told her. 'The time, the place . . . chosen.' And slowly, 'Listen to my mantra, you'll understand. You'll feel better too. "Through love I serve all life . . .

21

human, animal, the earth itself . . ." '

The words flowed around her, gentle, a cloak enfolding her. He went on, 'I have other mantras. I'll tell them to you, and you can choose which one you want.'

That was when he told her his name. 'Jake Babbitt. That's me.' And asked her hers.

She murmured, 'Elianne.'

They drove in silence for a little while, then he told her that she'd better plan on going along with him. It wasn't good for her to travel alone, she being so young. He said he was going back to New Mexico. To Taos. A place, he guessed, she'd never heard of.

'New Mexico,' she repeated. 'Oh, but I have heard of it.' And now she was excited. He must be right. This meeting had been meant to be. For New Mexico was where her Uncle Ian had lived, the uncle who had died before she was born. Her mother had spoken of him. How he had worked at Los Alamos during the Second World War, and was killed by a hit and run driver in Santa Fe.

Jake listened as she explained. 'Kill City. That's what we call Los Alamos. Our place is Love City.'

'Love City.' She tried out the words. They were sweet on her tongue.

'Through love I serve all life . . . human, animal, and the earth itself,' Jake said. And:

'Now you say it.'

Tears stung her eyes. It was meant to be. She had sought freedom to find Jake Babbitt. To find love. She was certain of it. She said, 'Yes, Jake. I'll go with you.'

Then the van swerved to the side of the road. He led her into the back. She had a quick glance of the van's side. A black sheen, a yellow rising sun, with golden rays spilling from it. And below it, in letters that seemed to drip like melted candles, *Love Is Divine.*

Within the van, he said. 'You know there's no free rides in this life, don't you?'

She was rigid with fright suddenly.

But Jake told her not to be scared. He said he wouldn't hurt her. He'd never hurt her.

He pulled off the cap she wore to conceal her shorn hair, her father's brutal handiwork, the last of those many hurts that had driven her from home. She ducked down, face ablaze.

Jake told her not to be ashamed. He fingered her hair, some short bristles, some matted and shaggy. He asked how it had happened.

And as she whispered, 'My father . . .' Jake spread his fingers wide to cup her head, to stroke and warm it. Then he opened her pants, and slid his hand down between her thighs to the silken curls that covered her mound. He twisted them around his fingers and gathered them into small peaks, then he smoothed

23

them. Soon he unbuttoned her shirt. Her breasts were small, round. He put his lips to each tiny nipple, his beard falling like a cashmere scarf along her shoulders as he kissed her throat before kissing the short bristles in her armpit. Laughing, he told her, 'You've got plenty of hair. Just let it grow, and you'll be okay.'

Then he was covering her, and in her, pumping hard with his hips, burrowing deeper with every thrust. She felt only momentary pain. It passed. She was lifted, floating. She thought she would explode and blow up into death.

Suddenly he reared away, his body a bow around its shaft, and she felt impaled on him. 'Wait!' he cried. 'Don't move! Tell me your name again. I can't fuck you if I don't remember your name.'

She gasped, 'Elianne.'

He misheard her. 'Ella,' he said. 'Ella Em.'

Then they were belly to belly, mouth to mouth, hip to hip, bodies striving. Finally the world shattered. Together they fluttered in empty space before slowly drifting into sleep.

Later, when she awakened, she remembered. She thought it only right that she should have a new name. She had found a new life. Ella Em. She liked the sound of it then.

Lying beside him, and hoping for his touch

again, she thought that she must love him because how else could she have such pleasure in him? But, as time passed, she learned that what she had felt with him wasn't love. And that she could know the same joy with other men, men Jake gave her to.

But now he whispered, 'My love opens the gates to life.'

They seemed to her, then, the truest words she'd ever heard.

Two weeks later, on the fourth of April 1968, the day, she knew now, on which her father had died, she and Jake were in a small cafe in Santa Fe. The Beatles were singing on the radio. The music suddenly stopped. Someone shouted that Martin Luther King had been shot in Memphis, Tennessee.

There was an instant hum of talk. People pressed close to each other. But Jake pushed back his chair. 'Come on, Ella Em. Let's get out of here.' His face was pale. His hair and beard looked wild. He dragged her outside, ignoring her anxious questions.

He climbed as if pursued into the van. He drove blindly, heading for Love City, for sanctuary.

The road snaked through the snow-covered hills. Always climbing, the van chugged and coughed.

Elianne leaned against Jake, watching the

glimmer of red rock, the squat pinion trees, their green limbs coated with glistening ice.

As they slowly inched up the long narrow looping horseshoe curve toward the pass at the top of Pilar Hill, a pickup truck came up behind them. Its horn blared, raucous and commanding. Jake smiled within his beard.

The pickup pulled out and passed them, its windows open. Three young men leaned toward them shouting obscenities. A hail of beer cans beat a sudden tattoo on the van.

Jake made the peace sign. The driver gave him the finger, shouting, 'Fucking hippies!'

'Welcome to Taos Valley,' Jake said, laughing.

It was like a bad dream. And just as suddenly over. Elianne let her breath out slowly. They were in the pass, then beyond. The valley spread out below them. Small houses with chimneys breathing blue puffs of smoke were scattered across it. The gorge of the Rio Grande River looked, from there, like a jagged black scar gouged out of the golden earth.

By then she had already begun to think of herself as Ella Em. A new name for a new life. She had come so far that the memory of home was fading. She was Ella Em, who chewed the magic mushroom, and smoked pot, and dropped acid on occasion. Ella Em, who followed where Jake led, who believed

in him, who thought that peyote and marijuana and LSD would keep her, as a mother
keeps her child with milk, at his side.

Then Jake said, 'Say it, Ella Em.'

Still staring into the valley, she said, ' "I see
the Divine in every person. I am in tune with
destiny and with myself, because I love." '

'We're almost to Love City.' he told her.

He rolled a cigarette, lit up and took a deep
drag, exhaling slowly.

She watched him. She already knew the
rules. It was always his turn first. Then,
maybe, it would be her turn. Maybe. She could
only hope.

Finally he grinned, and allowed her one
deep lungful of potent smoke before he took
the roach back. Sucking on it, he let the van
drift down the long hill that led into the valley,
to Ranchos de Taos, then Taos itself, and beyond it to the ancient pueblo, and beyond all
three to the place he called Love City.

Elianne remembered how she had savoured
the languor that spread through her, breathing
deeply of the sweetish air in the van. Soon she
smiled. The valley, the sky, were aglow . . .

She looked down the slope through the tendrils of the wistaria vine, eyes veiled with
tears. For the first time, she noticed the lit
windows of the cottage. Once it had been the
play room, where her father played pool with

Gordon and David.

Now her mother lived there with Ollie Duvaney.

Elianne sighed as she turned away from the window. It was time to throw away her backpack, to clean up and dress. Time to begin her new life in Hannah's Gate.

In the cottage, Ollie Duvaney said, 'Tell me about it. How did it go, Claire?' He held her tightly. To her, his warmth and tall, slender body were strength.

'It was wonderful,' she said. 'But, Ollie . . . oh, it was so hard. I mean, to tell her about Leigh and my mother. It was so . . . I didn't think she could take any more. I didn't mention Keith, nor what happened to him. I didn't say a word about Brett. She was always so fond of them both. And Brett was good to her.'

'There'll be time enough after she's had some rest.'

'Yes. She's very tired. I think she must have come a long way. The last word I had about her was Missouri, but she probably left there, else we'd have found her.'

'She'll tell you all about it, Claire. When she's ready.' He waited, but Claire didn't answer. He turned her face up to his. His eyes were bright, expressive. 'You *did* speak of me?'

'Oh, my darling, of course I did. You mustn't worry. That part of it will be fine. She has only to see you, to meet you . . . Oh, yes.' Claire smiled. 'Believe me, that part of it will be fine.'

'I hope so. I want her to like me, Claire. I want her to trust me.'

She smoothed back his thick grey hair. 'She will come to love you, Ollie. As I do.'

The cottage was different from when Leigh and the boys had played ping pong and pool and worked the pinball machines there, listening to World War II songs on the old juke box. All those things had been moved to a room in the new wing of the house a month before, when Claire and Ollie moved in.

She had furnished it with odds and ends from the house. A bedroom set that had been in the room used long ago by her brother Ian. A carpet from the living room, replaced when Leigh installed a new one. A sofa from the study. The book of Elizabeth Barrett Browning's love poems was moved to the bedside table in the bedroom that she and Ollie shared.

He kept the place filled with flowers that he bought several times a week on Wisconsin Avenue. It had become a refuge for them, a much needed one. Gordon and David resented Ollie's new position in the household. They were both doggedly polite, the surface courtesy only serving to underscore their unspoken rejection of him, and their unvoiced reproaches to Claire for having married him.

One day they had dug up the old World War II records that Leigh had liked. Now they played them repeatedly, so that for hours at a time, one or another of Leigh's favourite songs would resound through Hannah's Gate.

Claire ignored the boys' behaviour, but Ollie tried to be understanding. He was good to her nephew Keith, and had quickly won his friendship. It was Ollie who had suggested the lift that made it so much easier for Keith to get around in his wheel chair. Although nothing Ollie did penetrated the wall of reserve Gordon and David had built up around them, Claire felt certain that he would find Elianne happy to accept him as part of her family. Still, she was deeply troubled. Her mother's heart told her that, in those three years away, Elianne had been deeply hurt. She had come back profoundly changed. What had happened to her?

Now, looking into Ollie's smiling face, she tried to quell her uneasiness. 'We're together, you and I. And I have my family, all my children, with me at last.'

In the playroom, David leaned on a pool cue, pensively biting his lower lip. He and

Gordon had been discussing Elianne. Their reactions to her were much the same as they had been to Ollie. To both they showed one face. To each other, they showed another.

Gordon said, 'Why do you think she came home? What does she want? What makes her think she belongs here any more?'

David answered, 'She never did. Even though Mama always favoured her. God knows why. She never was very much. And look at her now.' David, usually silent, had no trouble talking with Gordon.

'She's the worse for wear. That's what it is,' his brother answered.

'If it wasn't for her, Dad would still be alive. Isn't that what you told me? I mean, back then, back when he died.'

'I guess I did tell you that. It's the truth. Dad always drank too much, but it was because he was worried about her. He couldn't stop thinking about how she ran away. About what she was doing, and where she was. How she'd bring disgrace on our name. Worry made him drink. He couldn't help himself. And the drinking killed him.'

'So, it *is* all her fault,' David murmured. He went on, 'And Ollie. Why did he come here? I thought we were finished with him when we left London.'

Gordon understood the connection that led

David to Ollie. Elianne was an intruder, always had been. Ollie was too. He and his brother had talked about Ollie many times before. Elianne and Ollie didn't belong here, and shouldn't pretend they did. Hannah's Gate was theirs. His and David's. Nobody else's.

'I guess Ollie came because of the money,' Gordon told David.

'He's got lots of his own. He doesn't need ours.'

'Maybe it's not true that he has. Maybe it's all lies. Plenty of English lords are poor. He could be one of them. Lord Creighton, the pauper, ready to feather his nest at our expense.'

'What can we do?' David asked glumly.

'Nothing,' Gordon told him. He rose, strode angrily around the room. He picked up a ping pong bat and smashed it down on the table. It splintered with a sharp crack. 'But that's what I'd like to do. Smash him!'

David said nothing. He punched a button on the juke box, turned the volume up high. Soon the room and the house echoed with *The White Cliffs of Dover*.

The last time the boys had had a similar conversation, Gordon had said, 'I'd like to tear him to pieces.'

And a few nights later, Claire and Ollie went to the National Theatre. They parked Ollie's

32

new car in the next door garage. When they returned to it, the convertible top had been cut from its frame. The seats had been sliced to ribbons.

The attendants had seen nothing, heard nothing. The incident was reported to the police, but Ollie never heard from them. He had the car repaired, and forgot about it.

Days later Gordon took David to Duke Zeibert's for an elaborate dinner. When they had finished huge portions of strawberry shortcake, Gordon said, 'We'll have to do this more often,' and added, 'Whenever we have reason to, that is.'

This time, a short while after Gordon said he'd like to smash Ollie just as he'd broken the ping pong bat, something else happened.

Ollie had brought home a large box of ten gardenia plants, each one in its own clay pot. He left the box on a table on a back terrace. When he came to retrieve it, the table lay on its side. The box was upended; the clay pots and their fragile gardenias were all crushed and scattered.

Days later Gordon took David to O'Donnell's, where both boys had huge bowls of mock turtle soup and a two and a half pound lobster apiece.

The same night Gordon and David spoke

of her and Ollie in the playroom, Elianne turned out the lamp beside her bed, and snuggled into her pillows. The room was dark, silent, except for the familiar sound of the wistaria vine. She was home.

They had all come together in the living room, before dinner. She had had only to see her mother with Ollie Duvaney to realize that Claire had finally found happiness. And Elianne knew, she was certain of it, that she herself had found a new friend.

Seeing her cousin Keith had been a shock. It was a good thing her mother had told her what to expect. Even so Elianne wasn't prepared for the sight of his useless legs, dangling against the footrest of his wheel chair. She didn't yet know how he had come to be paralyzed from the waist down. She hadn't wanted to ask. Her mother hadn't explained.

Keith didn't refer to his being crippled, except obliquely. He said, introducing her to his companion, 'This is Hank Ramos, my friend. He's also my teacher. He's been with me for a couple of months now and I wonder how I managed without him.'

Hank was twenty-four years old, a veteran of the Vietnam War. He had served for nearly two years in the infantry. He was tall, very slim, with olive skin, black hair and brilliant aquamarine eyes. His colouring, Elianne later learned, reflected his family heritage. His mother had been American, his father Puerto Rican. When Keith introduced him, Hank had given her a distant nod, a long unsmiling look.

She had felt herself recoil. It was as if he could see inside her. As if he knew where she'd been, what she'd done when her name was Ella Em.

As she drifted into sleep, she told herself to forget about Ella Em. Her name was now Elianne.

Chapter Two

Elianne awakened suddenly. For a few moments she didn't know where she was. The room was unfamiliar, its cool white walls seemed as transparent as mist. The pale curtains appeared to writhe, snakes dangling from iron bars. Her dreams were still fresh in her mind . . .

The mountain, its bald peak a red glow in the light of the rising moon. A ragged line of hills black against the flushed sky. Jake Babbitt's voice, chanting, 'I offer my heart to the Divine, which I love. I offer my love to the Divine . . .' The mountain. And Jake's deep voice. And sudden showers of sparkling glass dancing in the air like embers from an out of control fire.

The dream was actually memory. The fire had been real. Elianne had been seated near it, one of the group listening to Jake. Her hair was braided into a single rope tied at the end with a bit of faded ribbon, and fell to below

36

her shoulder blades. It had grown that much in the nearly three years since her father cut it off so close to her scalp that pink skin had shone through. She wore a long bedraggled skirt, its unfinished hem spewing a fringe of loose threads around her bare ankles. Her shoes were sneakers, marked with stains of kerosene and ash, and spattered with charred holes.

A little while before, the sun had set so that it was cold now. There was a faint blur of crimson on the horizon. Above it, blue twilight lay on the shoulders of the mountains, where aspen flared October yellow amid stands of blue spruce.

There were nine of them. Nine of Jake's people. And the three children. The oldest, Peace, was five, an adventurous boy. The middle one was Jonah, four, and timid. The baby was Joy, a curious three year old. Peace had a mother and father. Jonah had only a mother, Joy too. But the children belonged to all nine of them. That was what Jake had said. That was how it was.

'I am in tune with destiny and myself because I love. My being is focused on the Divine as I love everyone I know.'

Jake's religion. The creed of Babbitt, which he preached daily, full-throated and passionate, his black eyes blazing.

The war in that year, 1970, continued in Vietnam. American soldiers were accused of having massacred Vietnamese civilians in Mylai two years before. At Kent State, students were shot down on their campus. Black militants, and a judge they had taken hostage, were killed in a police roadblock. Anti-war activists bombed the Army Mathematics Research Centre at the University of Michigan, and a graduate student was killed.

But in the small commune Jake had established, he preached love and peace, and believed in them.

They had built small cabins, using their bare hands and the few tools they could borrow. They dug an earthen house into the side of a hill. It had skylights to allow in the sun by day, starlight by night. It was made of tin cans, stone, and dirt. It was Jake's house, and his church.

For a while Elianne had lived there with him, but then he chose another girl to share his place with him. Elianne moved to one of the cabins. It didn't matter. She was Ella Em, and her body belonged to anyone who wanted it. If she found brief joy at the moment of connection, that was fine. But she had quickly learned not to expect it. All she wanted was to be part of Jake's family.

With the October twilight deepening

around her, she became aware of the children. Peace was running in large circles around the open fire. Jonah trotted after him, shrilling wordlessly. Small Joy staggered after the other two, beating the air with tiny fists.

Jake was preaching. The group had been in town that day, selling hand-sewn moccasins and beadwork belts in the shops. In some places they were greeted kindly, but in many, they were insulted. And a man on the street had spat at them, reminding Elianne of the rattle of beer cans on the side of Jake's van, of the fast-moving pickup truck racing along beside them . . . Their arrival in Taos.

Jake, with his words, was trying to wash his family clean, to soothe its bruised feelings. 'The love pouring from me to you shall open the gate,' he said softly. 'The will to love shall open the gate. It will be the same for them. They hate us because we have chosen to live in the poverty to which they feel condemned. They hate us because we have chosen to come here for our souls' sake, when they want to go to the outside world for their greed's sake. But one day they too will find love, and the gate will be opened for them.'

The group stirred. Jonah's mother was laughing loudly. She rose up on her knees, leaned forward. The boy who had been sitting beside her, pulled her full skirt up, and mounted her from the back. She threw up her head, blonde hair trailing over his face and shoulders. He curved over her, his hips pumping.

Jake was silent, smiling. He looked above them towards the distant mountain, to Taos Mountain and said, 'My love is all, because I live in the spirit of the Divine. Love me. Love the Divine.'

The couple rocked to completion with loud groans. Then falling apart, they sedately took their places in the half-circle. The children continued to face the fire. Jake resumed his preaching.

The family worked for its survival. It had nothing except the members' few pieces of clothing, and some books they shared. Elianne knew nothing about the others, as they knew nothing about her. They all assumed that each had a reason for being there, and none of them cared what that reason was.

Five-year-old Peace discovered a ladder that leaned against the earthen house. He climbed it nimbly, stepped out on the slanted roof, dodged a skylight, and did a small dance above the doorway. Jonah struggled up the ladder, staggered to stand beside the boy. Joy stroked the bottom rung and sang to herself for a second or two before slowly dragging herself up. When she reached the roof, she stepped out blithely to join the boys. One step, two, and on the third, there was a loud crash. She hung briefly in empty space, flapping her arms as if they were wings to bear her aloft. But then, in a shower of sparkling glass, she fell.

Jake's voice went silent. There was only a soft tinkling nearby.

Joy lay on the dirt floor, legs sprawled, arms outflung. She was motionless, every inch of her exposed flesh aglitter with tiny shards of glass. Her dress was cut, and fell around her in ribbons, and more splintered glass sparkled between the shreds. As Elianne bent to gather her up, the tiny wounds began to ooze blood.

Within Elianne's arms, the child was cold. Her head fell limp on her neck. Her arms and legs drooped. She became the shattered doll that Elianne had once found lying on her bed, while Gordon, spying on her from the doorway, chuckled softly, and David stared at her with wide empty eyes.

As if from far away, Jake's voice came again, giving the lessons of the day. 'I am love, therefore I am divine. We are all divine because we love.'

The others chimed in, 'Because we love.'

Elianne heard the words, words she had believed in until this moment. Now they meant nothing to her. She held the small girl in her arms, and said, 'What am I doing here?'

It was too much to remember. Sighing, she flung back the sheets and quilt. She sat up. She promised herself that she wouldn't dream, she wouldn't remember. She had made the same promise repeatedly since her return to Hannah's Gate two months before.

She wouldn't dream. She wouldn't remember. She was herself now, and sane, and in the place where she belonged. She was home.

She wondered how long it would take to put the past truly behind her. The past, and Jake Babbitt. And the drugs she had so willingly taken into her body? Their sensations and their effects on her. Why? What had she done? When would there be an end to the sudden memories that sometimes floated up, seemingly from nowhere to assault and shame her. Who was that stranger she had called Ella Em for so long?

She dressed for the day thinking how odd it was that no one, none of those who had known her before, not her two brothers, not Keith, not even her mother, realized how much she had changed. As she remembered herself, she had been brave, demanding her freedom, certain she was entitled to make her own choices.

She had returned home timid, fearful, a prisoner of old memories, with hardly a will of her own. She felt that coming back had used up all her strength. Now there was nothing left.

Her mother had suggested that she study for her high school equivalency certificate so that she could enter college. Elianne immediately signed up for courses. Her mother had taken her shopping and picked out a wardrobe for her. She had shed the jeans and long skirts she had worn before without a thought. She had no opinions, and no judgement. She felt nothing but a dogged determination to hang on until she found her lost self again.

From outside her door, she heard the sound of Keith's wheel chair. She reminded herself that no matter how hard it was for her, it was harder still for him. By now, he had told her how he had come to be paralyzed.

It was a beautiful May morning at Kent State, where he had been a student. He'd been in the library, and was returning home with a load of books. There were demonstrations that day, mostly because American soldiers had just invaded Cambodia, when President Nixon had said 150,000 troops would be pulled out of the war soon. Keith saw the commotion . . . the kids yelling . . . stones flying . . . heard the curses . . . the ringing of the Commons bell . . . A group of National Guardsmen were chasing some students . . .

the kids throwing rocks . . . shouting filth at them too. A lot of students were just standing around, watching and laughing. The sun was so bright. Even the clouds of tear gas looked brilliant. Then a few of the guardsmen backed up a hill. The next thing Keith knew they had dropped to one knee, in firing position, with their guns up. Keith ran. He couldn't believe it when he heard the shots. He felt as if he'd been kicked in the back. And then he was on the ground, and a girl was screaming . . .

Elianne looked at her watch. It was seven-thirty, almost time to leave for her class. She picked up her bag, and went downstairs.

As the days passed, as the weeks became months, Elianne grew uneasy. She sensed a recognizable tension in the house. It had been the same when she was a child. Her father and the boys against her mother and Elianne herself. Only now it included Ollie.

Claire too sensed the tension. She told herself that as the boys grew more mature, they would understand that her love for Ollie didn't mean that she loved them less.

Ollie impinged on no one. He accepted the Merrill family routine as if it were his own. Claire was happy with him. Their love-making was sweet, life-giving. She wanted nothing

44

more than that they go on together, in the same way, forever.

If she worried about Gordon and David sometimes, she was pleased with Keith, who was making fine progress with his studies under Hank Ramos' guidance, and with Elianne, who seemed happy at home, and working hard to earn her high school credits. Claire knew that it wasn't easy. Her initial concern had been borne out in many ways. Elianne had much adjusting to do, and much to deal with. But, with time, Claire felt sure that Elianne would be fine.

It was early May. In downtown Washington the streets were jammed with anti-Vietnam War protesters from every state in the union. All that morning police sirens wailed along the avenues, and bullhorns amplified orders at blocked intersections.

But it was quiet on Honey Locust Lane. The trees lining the road were thick with leaves. The magnolias sagged beneath the weight of heavy cream-coloured flowers. The wistaria-covered parts of the back windows of Hannah's Gate and the terraces were bright with yellow and white roses.

As Claire and Ollie walked hand in hand up the slope toward the back door, he said he would soon need to make a trip to London to see to some investments. He suggested she go with him. At first, she protested. She didn't want to leave Elianne, Gordon, David and Keith. At least not yet. But, when Ollie said they could fly over and that at most they would only be away for five days, she agreed. It was pleasant to think of going back to where he had first courted her, to remember their walks along the Serpentine and dinners at the Gay Hussar.

Ollie took a yellow rose from one bush, a white one from another. He handed them to her with a flourish, and a quick kiss on the lips. Soon afterwards, he left to go to a travel agent to set up the trip.

Claire watched him drive away. He was so good to her, and for her. She was lucky they had found each other, and that he had come here to Hannah's Gate, to her. Later, she pressed the two roses between the pages of a thick dictionary, and left it on the end table in the study.

She had a telephone conversation with Anna Taylor, who hadn't been well, then planned dinner menus for the week.

When she had finished her chores, she looked at the Washington *Post*. The front page was devoted to stories about the demonstrations. Some 300,000 people had taken part, among them a group of Vietnam War veterans. She wondered briefly what Hank Ramos thought about the protests. He had been there, she knew, but she'd never heard him mention the war.

She put the paper aside, leaned back in her chair. London. Oh, it would be nice to be there with Ollie again.

An hour later, moments after Elianne had returned home from the library and gone up to her room, she heard the hum of the lift and the clang of its door. Then Keith called, 'Hank! Where are you? I need you!' His voice was rough, frightened.

Alarmed, she went into the hall. 'What's wrong, Keith?'

Before he could answer, Hank was there. 'What's the matter?'

'Downstairs! It's Aunt Claire. She's sick, I think.'

'Wait here,' Hank said to Keith.

By then, Elianne had already started down. Hank passed her by, leaping the stairs three at a time.

Claire was in the study, lying in her chair, both hands pressed to the sides of her head. She was white-faced, gasping. 'My head,' she moaned. 'Oh Elianne . . . Hank . . . it . . .' And then, faintly, 'Ollie . . .'

Elianne called for an ambulance. In less than

ten minutes it pulled up before Hannah's Gate. It took only moments to wrap Claire in blankets and to carry her outside on a stretcher. By then she was parchment pale, scarcely breathing.

Elianne rode with her mother, holding her limp hand, whispering desperately, 'Oh, Mama, Mama, try . . .'

But Claire was dead by the time they reached the hospital.

An autopsy showed that Claire had died of an aneurysm in the brain. She had shown no symptoms of a problem beforehand, and once the weak artery gave way, nothing could have been done.

Ollie was grey-faced, choking back his grief.

Elianne moved in stunned silence through the tasks required of her.

Gordon and David were red-eyed and sombre.

Then, one day at the end of June, their lawyer gathered the family to read to it the will Claire had made immediately after Dora Loving died.

Talcott was middle-aged, with thick grey hair. He wore black-framed glasses and had a penchant for bowties, sporting a green and grey one that afternoon. He headed the firm of which Jeremiah Merrill had been senior partner years before.

Now he stood beneath the portrait of Big Jack Gowan and regarded the assembled family.

Irene Beston, no longer the young girl she had been when Leigh and Claire were married, passed round cookies and coffee. After Claire's death she had agreed to move in and keep house for Elianne and the others.

When she withdrew, Talcott cleared his throat.

Gordon leaned forward, while David stared at the floor.

Keith looked attentive. Hank, here in case Keith needed him, seemed to be thinking of something far removed.

Ollie Duvaney was expressionless, his face furrowed. In these past three weeks he had aged.

Elianne glanced at him. She wished there was some consolation to offer him. But she knew that she could say nothing that would make him feel less bereft.

Now Talcott was saying, 'I assure you that your mother was of sound mind, and as far as we knew, in good health, when this will was written.' He began to read, each syllable full and rounded, and spaced by pauses at every comma and period.

Slowly the provisions of the will became

clear to Elianne. The document was compli-
cated, covering a fortune in real estate and
stocks and bonds. Hannah's Gate, inherited by
Claire on her mother's death, was willed directly to Elianne. But Gordon and David and
Keith were given lifetime interests in the
house, and could live there as long as they
liked. Trusts were established for each of the
three boys, and for Elianne. As each turned
twenty-five, he would receive his share of the
principal. Elianne was to be administratrix of
the trusts. Foster Talcott would be the ex-
ecutor, and until Elianne reached twenty-one,
he would be co-executor with her.

When his soft voice stopped, a thick silence
fell on the room. Everyone stared at Elianne.

She felt the colour drain from her face. She
clutched the chair arms with trembling fingers. 'No,' she whispered. 'I can't do it!'

Gordon jumped to his feet. 'Now I know
why you came home! She told you, didn't she?
She bribed you into it. You knew about the
will all along.'

'Just a moment!' Foster Talcott snapped.
'Your mother's will was written after your
grandmother's death. Your mother didn't
know where Elianne was then. She'd heard
from her that she was returning home, but
Elianne hadn't yet arrived. There was no discussion between your mother and Elianne.'

Again there was a sullen silence.

David looked at the floor, his mouth working.

Gordon stared at Elianne, eyes glittering. Then, slowly, he regained his self-control. He managed a smile. 'I'm sorry, Elianne. I guess I was taken by surprise.'

Ollie put his arm around her. He said to Gordon, 'Your mother did exactly what she wanted to do, and what she thought was best.' He went on gently, 'We're all that's left.' His eyes moved from Gordon to David to Keith, and then, at last, to Elianne. 'We must take care of each other.'

'Yes,' Gordon agreed, while David stared at him.

Voice shaking, Elianne said, 'I'll do the best I can, but you'll have to help me. Okay?'

It was later that same day when Gordon told David. 'Come on. I want to show you something.' He led David into the lower hallway. 'Look at the chandelier. Isn't it beautiful?' When David nodded, Gordon went on, 'Dad said it was one of the best in the city.' His voice dropped. 'It should have been ours.' He took David to the living room. 'Dad picked out this carpet himself. He watched it laid. It should have been ours, David.'

Gordon took his brother on a complete tour

of Hannah's Gate. The dining room, the kitchen, the study, where earlier, beneath the portrait of Big Jack Gowan, the boys' great grandfather, Foster Talcott had read Claire Merrill's will.

Gordon led David to the bomb shelter, reminding him that Leigh had built it to save the family. He led his brother up the stairs past the place where, a generation before, a young girl named Linda Grant had been killed, and then showed him Hank Ramos' room, where Linda Grant had lived, and where she had dreamed her fantasy about a traitor named Logan Jessup. He showed David through Elianne's room, where Margo Desales had watched Logan Jessup from her window, and climbed through it for the trysts that led finally to her murder. He took David to the third-floor attic, now occupied by Irene Beston, where a woman who called herself Carrie Day had written her stories, while searching for the wealth she hoped Big Jack Gowan had left to her, all the time pretending to herself that she, not Dora Loving, was Big Jack's legal daughter, and the heiress to Hannah's Gate.

Then he took David down to the new wing. The guest rooms. The new play room. He punched a button on the juke box, and *I'll Walk Alone* came on. That song, he told David, had been Leigh's favourite. Each time they had walked a corridor, passed a door, Gordon said, 'This should all have been ours.' Now, while the music echoed around them, he said it again, 'This should have all been ours. It's what Dad made, and what he wanted. Hannah's Gate should have belonged to us.'

He pulled David through the whole property, from Honey Locust Lane to Afton Place, and finally he said, 'Elianne can't even take care of herself. How is she going to manage all this?'

David looked into his brother's eyes, waiting.

'And as for Ollie Duvaney, he's got nothing to do with it. He doesn't belong here. He's not a member of our family. The sooner he leaves the better.'

'But what are you going to do?' David asked.

'I don't know yet. I have to think about it.' Gordon answered. Then he stamped back to the house. David trailing him as if drawn on a string.

It soon became clear that there was no place for Ollie Duvaney in Hannah's Gate. Gordon and David stopped speaking to him. They ignored him, and his attempted pleasantries. When Elianne tried to talk to them about their behaviour, they walked away. That is, Gordon walked away, shoulders set. David followed, a tall silent shadow.

Elianne thought it might have been different if Ollie had had some authority or position in the household, but he didn't, a situation the boys exploited. This left Elianne always in the middle, a mediator to whom no one listened.

One day in late September when she returned from the new Kennedy Centre for the Performing Arts, Ollie was waiting for her. After she'd spoken about the show, and about the Centre, he drew her out to the terrace. His face was earnest, regretful. 'Elianne, I create more dissension here than I do good for you.'

It was no use pretending otherwise. She said, 'I'm still hoping that will change.'

'I wish I believed that it would. I want to be here. For your sake, and my own. Here I can still feel close to your mother.' His voice deepened, broke. When he went on, it shook. 'We had so little time together. So little time . . .' He paused. Then: 'But it's no use. I can't pretend that I'm needed at Hannah's Gate. Nor wanted. I think it will be better for all of us if I go. And you'll be all right. You're far stronger than you think.'

She wished it were true. She felt completely

overwhelmed. It had been like that ever since she returned home. It seemed much worse now that her mother was dead. Hannah's Gate was like a giant octopus, clutching her in invisible tentacles. She had escaped them once. She could never escape them again, she feared.

Ollie went on, 'You have Keith, and Hank Ramos. And if there's a serious problem, you can always depend on Foster Talcott.'

She wanted to beg Ollie to stay. She needed him there. But she felt that he had the right to his own life. She didn't want him to be sacrificed for her sake.

She said, trying to sound confident, 'We'll manage, Ollie.'

'Of course you will. And if you need me, just call. I'll come back immediately. From wherever I am. No matter what I'm doing.' He put into her hand, a thin volume. 'I want you to have these, Elianne. I gave them to your mother when she was in England.'

Elianne looked at the title. *Sonnets from the Portuguese.* She knew Claire had always kept the book on her bedside table. Her voice shook when she thanked Ollie.

A week later, he was gone.

Chapter Three

For the next four years all that happened beyond the walls that Leigh Merrill had built seemed distant to Elianne.

With Keith and Hank, she watched on television reports of Patricia Hearst's kidnapping by the Symbionese Liberation Army, and saw sequences of huge anti-war demonstrations. She saw photos of the men arrested for breaking into the Democratic Committee's offices in the Watergate building. In November of 1972, she kept track of the election returns when Richard Nixon was re-elected, and listened to interviews outside the courthouses where the Watergate burglars were tried. Two years later, along with the rest of the country, she saw the impeachment hearings, and in August she saw the president make his farewell speech at the White House after his resignation.

Yet all the while she felt as if she were living in a dream. She received her high school equivalency certificate and entered college. With the help of the housekeeper, Irene Beston, she ran the house, attempting to maintain a semblance of family life for her brothers and Keith, knowing that was what Claire had hoped for.

Prey to her memories of Jake Babbitt and her life with him, she tried to come to terms with her immediate past. Why had she thought Jake's words were true? Why had she followed him into what she now found so hard to accept? She supposed she had needed to belong somewhere, to someone. She had needed to believe in love. Then she had seen the baby called Joy fall through the skylight, and had known clearly and painfully that there was no love in Love City. So she had fled the drug-dulled days, and come home. But nightmare dreams had come with her. There were long moments when she was uncertain what had been real, what had been imagined.

Her brothers remained polite but distant, their resentment that she had inherited Hannah's Gate silent yet palpable. Gordon graduated prep school, but refused to continue his education, in spite of Elianne's pleas and Foster Talcott's lectures. David was still in his senior year. Both boys had their own lives beyond Hannah's Gate, and came and went as they pleased.

Her only ally was Keith. Soft-spoken, smiling Keith, who went about the house in his wheel chair, used the lift, studied with Hank a good part of every day, and still had time for Elianne. Thus Hank and Elianne were thrown together too.

Gradually she became aware of him as a person, a man. It happened slowly. She never knew exactly when she realized that he was attractive, noticed how deep his voice was and found herself listening for it. She was aware of how his head tipped sideways when Keith spoke to him, how he moved his body with grace. Over time she sensed that he was beginning to see her with new eyes too. His gaze followed her when she moved about the room. She wondered if he thought of her when he was alone with Keith.

Early in January 1975, on a grey windy morning, Hank hurried into the dining room where Irene had set up breakfast, as was the custom. Keith, he said, had a fever.

She was instantly alarmed. Keith had always been well, vigorous. He couldn't move from his chair, couldn't get out of bed without help, yet he'd never even had a cold. Except for the paralysis that affected him from the waist down, he was as healthy as any twenty-five year old.

She telephoned the doctor, then went upstairs. Something was obviously wrong with Keith. His eyes glittered. Although his cheeks were flushed, his lips were pale. He tried to smile at her. She told him to rest, and went into the hall, Hank following her.

'I can't believe it,' she whispered. 'He seemed fine last night.' She was remembering her mother. Claire had been happy and vigorous. And then suddenly, within moments . . .

'Except that he said he was tired and wanted to go to bed earlier than usual.' Hank's voice was soft, his expression worried. 'I should have known then.'

She said, 'I'm scared, Hank.'

'He'll be okay.' Hank tried to sound confident, but he was frightened too. He knew that whatever was wrong with Keith would only be made worse by his disability.

Within the hour they knew that Keith had pneumonia. The doctor insisted that he be moved to the hospital, although both Hank and Elianne said they could get nurses in and care for him at home. That was when the doctor explained that he wanted Keith close to the best equipment: A respirator, blood transfusion apparatus. It was a matter of being prepared, just in case, the doctor said.

Soon after, an ambulance took Keith to the hospital. Hank rode with him. Elianne followed in her Toyota.

It was two weeks before Keith was out of danger and on the mend. Another two weeks before he was brought home.

Elianne and Hank spent all their time with him. They sat with him when he was awake. When he slept they walked slowly up and down the corridors. They spoke little. Elianne, however, was very aware of Hank's gentle and caring nature. She had never known a man like him. She found herself comparing him to her father, to Jake, to the other men she'd known. She asked herself if what she saw of Hank was real, or if it was a mask he wore, concealing behind it another Hank.

She managed to keep up with her school work, getting lecture notes from Stacy Grayson, a girl who sat beside her in class.

When Keith was home, he seemed different. He was content as never before, to remain in bed, rather than go about the house in his wheel chair. He spent more time in his room, alone with Hank, than he had before his illness.

The doctor said his slow recovery was to be expected. But, by the end of March, Elianne was concerned. Hank agreed, suggesting that a change of scenery might help.

A few days later, Elianne came upon a magazine article about Death Valley in eastern

California. Pictures showed a wild and desolate place. A resort called Furnace Creek Inn was described.

Hank didn't know the hotel, but he had been to Death Valley years before with his parents. His eyes glowed when he told Elianne about the hot dry air and the cloudless blue skies.

That afternoon she spoke of the place to Keith. It had a pool filled by a hot springs. There was a lift. The grounds were beautiful. She asked if he'd like to pay a visit there.

He agreed listlessly, and two weeks later, Elianne and Keith flew to Las Vegas. There they were met by Hank, who had driven Keith's special van across country to meet them.

From Las Vegas it was a three-hour drive to Death Valley. They passed through tiny towns, crossed small oases of tamarisk trees amid long miles of rolling empty terrain. Exotic Joshua trees grew in scattered groves, and Spanish bayonet, and beavertail cactus glistened in the sun. Hank excitedly named these plants as they passed them by. Then the van laboured up cedar-covered hills, finally reaching golden canyons and mustard-coloured cliffs. Emerging from them, the three saw Furnace Creek Inn, set in another oasis, but this time with royal palms and oleander, and, when they went to look closer, they found velvet green lawns terraced to a small pond. The pool was nearby, but a full level below the lift. Hank found an attendant who assured him of help with Keith's chair whenever it was needed.

Keith, looking about him, was suddenly joyful. 'This place looks like the foyer to heaven! I'm glad we came.'

Hank glanced sideways at Elianne at the same time that she looked at him. Their eyes met. A quick thrill went through her. She had no time then to examine her feelings, but later she remembered that leap of excitement, and realized that some small dead place inside of her had come alive.

Within days, Keith began to improve. He spent the mornings swimming. Afternoons, when it was too hot for him to be out, they got into the air-conditioned van and drove around the valley. They saw the great salt flats called the Devil's Golf Course that stretched for water-like shining miles. They chased skipping mirages down the narrow roads, where wild burros watched as they went by. They visited Salt Creek, and Hank pushed Keith in his wheel chair along the boardwalk, pausing at tiny pools where minute pupfish spawned and swam. At Zabriskie Point they marvelled at the play of light over the wind-carved hills, the glint of mica, and white limestone, the green that was copper. The valley was enclosed by the Grapevine and Funeral Mountains to the east, and to the west, the Panamints.

The sky above was a sharp blue, with occasional white trails left by military planes from bases miles away.

Often the three of them stopped to examine enclaves of wild flowers. Miniature purple stars sprinkled through veins of gravel at the side of the road, clumps of wild blue asters.

Twice they drove through lavender twilight to Death Valley Junction to see Marta Beckett perform in her Amargosa Opera House, where, in days when she had had only a few come to see her art, she had painted the walls with a lavishly costumed audience of lords and ladies and peasants and gypsies, for whom she could dance and pantomime. Now, though, the seats were full, the applause long and enthusiastic.

As Keith grew stronger, Hank and Elianne marvelled at the colour in his face, the strength in his arms. Their shared interest and concern for him drew them closer than they had ever been.

But Elianne realized it was more than that for her. Hank was always in her thoughts. When she lay at the side of the pool, listening to Hank and Keith talking, she found herself picturing Hank's face. His dark blue eyes, slightly slanted at the corners, with their faintly Oriental look. His crisp dark hair. The sudden flash of his smile, lighting his usual sober expression.

It had been a long time since she had thought she loved Jake Babbitt. But she remembered how she had felt then. It was the same now. She trembled at the sound of a voice. But it was Hank's. She yearned for the touch of a hand. But it was Hank's touch. Yet he was matter-of-fact with her, friendly but no more. That made her determined to conceal her own feelings.

Then, one night, after Keith had gone to bed, she went for a walk down the steep hill that led to the main road.

A shadow broke away from the puddle of darkness beneath a tree. 'Elianne?' Hank fell into step beside her. 'Keith's in bed, reading. Is it okay if I come with you?'

'Sure,' she said casually, determined that he should not realize how deeply his nearness affected her. Just walking beside him she felt wrapped in a tender warmth.

Their two shadows fell before them, moving along the empty road. The sky arched over them, endless and black, but shining with the silver band of the Milky Way. At the peak of Telescope Hill a single light burned white and still. A coyote keened from a distant slope. Moments later another responded.

'It's going to be hard to leave this place,' Hank said.

'It will be for me.' She thought of Hannah's Gate, of David and Gordon. Oh, how she wished that the boys weren't her responsibility. She didn't know how to deal with them. Though they never spoke of it, she knew how much they resented the will that had made them dependent on her. Her efforts to create stability, a family, seemed empty. She and Keith got along well, but the boys always tried to get him to side with them. He managed to stay friends with them, but how long could that go on? It was the same for Hank. And because it was below the surface, and never talked about, it was all the more difficult. She shivered, thinking of Gordon whispering to David, of David laughing.

There was a stone in the road that she didn't see. She struck it with the toe of her sneaker. It rolled away, but she staggered, nearly fell.

Hank's arm came around her. Even when she was steadied on her feet, he held her. He whispered, 'I've wanted to do this for a long time. Ever since you came home . . .' He dipped his head to kiss her eyes, her cheeks, then her mouth. Softly, then harder. With passion. She clung to him, unable to speak.

They moved off the road into the shadows of the rocks. There, in a nest of stone still warm from the hot daytime sun, they slipped from their clothes and lay naked in each other's arms, their hearts beating together, blood singing through them, and finally, joined and straining, limbs locked, arms clenched, mouths sealed in a kiss, they reached oneness.

Later, in her room, Elianne unwillingly sponged the sand of the desert from her skin. It was part of their love. She knew now that she had never known love before. Jake, the others she had known, had barely touched the well-spring of her heart through the barrier of her drug-blunted senses. She would never compare what she had known then to what she had known tonight. Ella Em was dead. Elianne was new, made whole.

In her reflection, she saw shining eyes, a faint smile. Unconsciously her hands went to her long hair. 'I'm me,' she whispered. 'Elianne.'

For the next two weeks, after Keith had retired, Hank and Elianne met nightly. They lay in each other's arms, pretending that they would always be in Death Valley, encircled by the protective mountains.

In the mornings, before Keith rose, they

met for coffee in the lobby, and watched television news together. They saw a brief report on the bombing of Fraunces Tavern in New York City by men believed to be Puerto Rican nationalists. Another time the events of the Bicentennial Era, which had started that month, were described. Often the news and weather reports passed in a blur, while they were aware only of each other.

Except for those interludes they were with Keith. Although they never touched, never spoke of their feelings to him, he soon realized what had happened, and was glad for them.

He knew Hank well, his strength and kindness. He knew Elianne too. He was three years older than her, and had only faint memories of her as a child. Images of her eyes, wide and glistening with tears when her father yelled at her. Images of her small shrinking form when Gordon teased her and David giggled. He understood her sense of aloneness. Momentarily he felt the same sense of loss he'd drowned in when he'd found his father, Brett, on the stairs of their Boston home, dead of a cerebral haemorrhage, only weeks after Keith had returned from the hospital in his wheel chair.

He had only the barest recollection of his mother. She had been named Rea. She was tall, with a waterfall of black hair and smooth white cheeks. He knew that she had turned away when he tried to stroke her face. Why had she left him? He didn't know that. His father had spoken of her only rarely, a shadow descending on his expression when he did. Keith knew that Rea had died in Mexico, but he didn't know what she was doing there. His Aunt Claire, his Grandmother Dora, had occasionally mentioned her, but she remained a mystery to him. So he knew what it was to be alone. He accepted his life. He didn't want a similar one for Elianne. His body was crippled, and couldn't be healed. Her soul had been crippled, but Keith believed it could be made well. So he was happy that she and Hank had discovered each other, and determined to do what he could to help them. When he thought of Gordon and David his hands clenched unconsciously. He knew them for what they were: spoiled children. Not David so much. Keith had realized long ago that David was hardly more than an empty vessel into which Gordon poured his feelings, making them David's feelings too. He got along with both boys because he was determined to. But now he was just as determined to give Elianne her chance for happiness and love.

The beautiful sunlit days came to an end. It was time to leave Furnace Creek Inn.

Keith insisted that he was well enough now to go with Hank in the van, so the two men put Elianne on a plane in Las Vegas and she flew to Washington. Then Hank and Keith set out on the four day journey for home.

Elianne arrived at ten o'clock that night. She took a cab to Hannah's Gate. As it pulled up before the house, she took a deep steadying breath. She had the same frightened, trembly feeling that she'd had when she first returned home five years before. The street was still. She saw that all the windows were dark except for a small glint of light from the top-floor attic room that was Irene's.

The magnolia tree was draped in black shadows. The bare limbs of the honey locust trees whispered overhead.

Perhaps Gordon and David were out. Or perhaps they were in one of the rooms at the back of the house, or in the new wing. She wished that Keith and Hank were with her.

Her hands shook when she unlocked the door. She stepped inside, closed it behind her. The silence was so noticeable that she heard only the sound of her own pulses in her ears.

'Anybody home?' she called.

There was no response.

Slowly, carrying her suitcase, she went up the stairs and into her room. It was dark and airless. She felt as if she couldn't breathe. She

69

turned on a small lamp, and opened the window. The wistaria scraped along the glass. She looked around the room. It was the same as always. Home, she thought. And everything's the same.

Then, suddenly, loud music rocked her. The juke box, volume turned as high as it would go, was playing *Pistol Packin' Mama*.

They were sitting side by side on the edge of the tarpaulin-covered pool. Gordon's full thighs felt the cold of the concrete sift through his heavy corduroy trousers. David's jacket was open, his shirt partly unbuttoned. He never noticed the weather. Heat or cold were same to him.

They had stopped playing the juke box and come out here at Gordon's suggestion. But he hadn't spoken for a long time. David didn't mind. When Gordon was ready, he'd say what he had to say.

At last, with a moody mulish expression, he said, 'God she makes me mad! It makes me want to kick her.' He looked up at the light in Elianne's window. 'Yes. She's back all right.' He was silent for a moment. Then: 'But the only thing that really worries me is how long she's going to lord it over us. I have to be twenty-five. Twenty-five, for Christ's sake! Before I get my inheritance. Six endless years.'

'And eight years for me,' David muttered.

'It's a long time,' Gordon said darkly. 'Anything could happen. To either one of us. If only Foster Talcott weren't such a jerk we could have made some arrangement with him, but the man's a fool.'

'A damn fool,' David agreed.

'And who knows? Maybe Elianne will get married.'

'What if she did?'

'Then her husband would get Hannah's Gate. If anything happened to her.'

'Her husband?' David echoed. Then: 'But maybe she'd go away.'

'No such luck. She's going to take care of Keith, and she's going to take care of you and me. Whether we want her to or not!' He laughed bitterly. 'She's decided it's her duty.'

'Yes,' David said. 'She thinks it's her duty to take care of us. Whether we want her to or not.' After a while, he asked, 'Then what are we going to do, Gordon?'

'I don't know,' Gordon answered. 'But I'm going to have to think of something.'

Chapter Four

The sounds of the old house were familiar. The squeak of Keith's wheel chair rolling down the hallway towards the lift, the faint patter of squirrels racing across the roof. But now Elianne listened for other familiar sounds: Hank's footsteps; the deep murmur of his voice as he spoke to Keith. Always, whenever he was in the house, she was aware of him. Always, she yearned to re-capture the warmth of those moments they had shared in Death Valley.

But since their return home several weeks before, they had had no time together. It was as if those wonderful days away had been a dream, and when she came back to Hannah's Gate she awakened into the reality of her life.

Still, there were moments when their eyes met, and she knew that he felt the same. At the table, on occasion, their hands touched briefly. An invisible current moved between them. It wouldn't have surprised her to see sparks flare up.

Now, as she dressed for dinner, she wondered how long it would be before he held her in his arms again. She knew the decision she and Hank had made in Death Valley to keep their affair secret was the right one, the only one to make. To reveal to Gordon and David how she felt about Hank would only introduce another complication.

It was already difficult to deal with them. Gordon complained that she didn't give him enough money, although the allowance Foster Talcott had suggested seemed more than ample. When she brought up the subject of college to Gordon, he said calmly, 'I'm finished with school. I don't see the need for it. I'd appreciate it if you'd mind your own business, and allow me to mind mine.' And when she told him that he drank too much, he stared at her, hot-eyed, flushed with anger, and didn't answer.

She knew she had to make Gordon, and David too, see that they were behaving like spoiled children. She thought of it often, planned her words, but when it was time to say them, she found that she couldn't. The boys were so forbidding, their faces hard as if carved from stone, their eyes filled with secret laughter.

She imagined Gordon would say, 'If you don't like it here, don't like us as we are, why don't you go away?'

But she had done that once. She'd run away from Hannah's Gate before, her hair shorn almost to the scalp, carrying only a few dollars and a change of shirts. She'd run away and become Ella Em.

The memory of that girl kept her from confronting Gordon and David. She had begun to remember her again, to dream of her, seeing once more the small girl falling through glittering shards to die on the hard earth, while around her, in a semi-circle, a group of uncaring adults listened to Jake Babbitt speak of love as divine.

Now Elianne blinked at her reflection in the mirror. She smoothed her hair one more time, and sighed, and went downstairs.

Keith and Hank were waiting. They went to the dinner table together. Irene had just begun to serve them when Gordon and David came in.

Gordon's eyes were, as often, too bright. A slight smile tugged at his lips. He settled his big body in his chair, looked around. 'A loving family meal,' he said.

David took his place without speaking.

Keith ignored Gordon's comment. He spoke of Death Valley, the dry air and the hot sun.

He said Gordon and David ought to visit there one day.

Hank mentioned Big Sur in California, too, another place the boys ought to see.

Gordon, who had been barely listening, suddenly paid attention. He turned to stare at Hank. 'When were you there?'

'A few years ago.'

'Before or after Vietnam?'

'Before,' Hank said briefly. 'Why do you ask?' His face was suddenly an Oriental mask, the eyes slightly slanted at the corners, now veiled, the hollows deeper beneath the cheek bones. He was wondering what to say, how to say it. He was wondering what Elianne would think. They had had so little time together, hardly enough to explore the wonder of finding each other, not nearly enough to join in an exploration of their pasts.

Gordon shrugged. 'I was just asking. It's occurred to me that we don't know anything about you.'

'What would you like to know?' Hank asked softly.

'Nothing, I guess,' Gordon muttered after a silent moment. 'You can say whatever you want to, can't you? How would I know the truth from a lie?'

Keith cut in before Hank could answer. He said, smiling, 'Stop that, Gordon. You're just picking on Hank, trying to get a rise out of him.'

Gordon's quick, sideways grin was forced. He finished his meal quickly and left the room.

David followed him almost immediately.

Keith said, 'Don't pay any attention to Gordon. You know how he is.'

'I know,' Hank said. 'It's okay. Don't worry about it.'

Easy to say those words, he thought later, as he and Keith watched television together. Not so easy to make them work. What was Gordon driving at? Why was he suddenly curious about Hank after all these years of taking him completely for granted?

When Claire hired him to come to Hannah's Gate to stay with Keith she had said it wasn't necessary to mention how they'd met. It meant nothing to him. Later he understood that she hadn't wanted to speak of the detective agency run by Charlie Carroll. Her search for Elianne had been private, at least as far as Hank could tell. No one had spoken of it, although he knew it continued to go forward actively until the day Elianne telephoned to ask if she could come home.

He still remembered the afternoon that Claire Merrill walked into the office on Fifteenth Street. Her dark raincoat was soaked through. Her auburn hair sparkled with rain-drops. He had guessed, even before she stated the reason for her coming, that it had to do with a runaway child. He told her that she would have to wait to talk to Charlie Carroll.

He hadn't wanted to hear about her trouble. He felt he had enough of his own. He'd arrived in Washington only a few weeks before, mostly because Charlie, whom he'd known in Vietnam, had suggested it. He'd been drifting, so he drifted east. When he came out of the hospital, there'd been no home to go to. The place on Big Sur that had been home was gone, his parents with it. While he was in the hospital there'd been long weeks of rain . . . the shifting of clay cliffs . . . the roar of collapse when everything below had been swept away and into the ocean. Nothing was left of the small inn, the grove of trees, the carefully tended flower beds.

That, and what had come before, had been more than enough for a twenty-two year old to deal with. So he'd drifted east, and stayed with Charlie, and Amy his wife. Hank dealt with the phone when Charlie was out, did some of the paper work. He didn't want to hear about Claire Merrill's troubles. Listening was Charlie's job, not his. But Charlie spoke of what he'd heard. She had had several agencies before, looking for her daughter Elianne.

No luck. The woman had to keep trying. Her husband had died recently. Her nephew was a cripple. Charlie dropped bits and pieces of what he heard. Eventually Hank began to listen. One day Charlie said, 'That woman needs help. Maybe it's something you should try.' Hank figured that Charlie and Amy were tired of putting him up, having him around. It was more to accommodate them than anything else that he offered to be a companion to Keith. That was the beginning.

It changed after he met Keith, and saw his need, and realized that he, Hank Ramos, could do a lot for him. Very soon he realized that in helping Keith, he was healing himself.

There had been a place called Bien Kok. A hot twilight. Grey, steamy air. A shallow river, edged with trees. He and Charlie, and the five others, had been pinned down for hours, with machine guns rattling around them. Torn leaves drifting down, splinters of wet bark, thick slimy leeches. Suddenly there was silence. Time to move on. They waded across the river and dodged into the shadows. Nothing. A scary quiet. They followed a track. Charlie behind the others. Hank at the end of the single file. Suddenly the trail dipped, widened. There were nine of them, a huddle of women, some carrying babies, some tiny children. Two old men. The men ahead fired on command. Fired. Fired. Screaming faces. blood. Burning smoke. The gun jerked in his hand, slammed into his shoulder.

They were all down. The old men. The women with their babies. The tiny children. Down in the shadows, the dust, the blood. Had he fired at the sky, aiming high? Or had he shot those killing bullets at them? He didn't know. He couldn't remember.

The seven soldiers went on. Nobody ever spoke of it. Nobody cared. But he dreamed of those few moments. He tried to recapture them, to remember. Over long months, he had taught himself that he mustn't try, mustn't remember. It couldn't be changed. But in helping Keith he began to feel that he was redeeming himself.

Elianne had also been troubled by the exchange at the dinner table. Gordon questioning Hank in that ugly sneering voice, his eyes narrowed with malice.

Later, in the bedroom, she went over it in her mind. She heard Gordon and David drive away. She heard Hank wheel Keith into his room. Several hours later, she heard Hank's footsteps in the hallway. The back door opened and closed. She guessed that he'd gone out, as she knew he sometimes did, after Keith was settled in bed.

When she looked from the window, she saw Hank walk slowly around the pool area, then sit on the steps to the cottage, once the playroom for the boys, then occupied so briefly by Claire and Ollie when they were married.

Watching Hank, she wondered how Ollie was. It had been some time since she'd heard from him. She wished he hadn't gone away, but knew that he'd felt he had to. His absence had changed nothing, although he'd meant it for the best. She thought about writing to ask him to return. But she decided it would be unfair to him. He had to make a new life for himself. He wouldn't do that here at Hannah's Gate.

Her mind went back to Gordon's questions. He had managed to drive Ollie away. Was he going to try to drive Hank away too? Is that what the little scene at dinner really meant?

She couldn't let it happen. Keith needed Hank. She herself needed Hank. She wondered what she could do to stop Gordon. There had to be a way. There had to . . .

Hank stirred, tipped back his head. He was looking up at her window. Was he remembering their time together at Furnace Creek Inn?

A wave of longing swept her. Oh, how she needed him, wanted him. She knew David and Gordon had gone out, having heard the car pull away. Keith must be sleeping by now. Irene was at the top of the house in her own little room, probably immersed in a television show.

Elianne snatched a light coat from the closet and ran downstairs.

Hank rose as she approached him. 'Elianne . . .'

'I saw you out here, and I . . .' She didn't finish the sentence. He had enclosed her in his arms, pulled her to him. His kiss swallowed the rest of her words.

After that, they didn't speak. He led her into the cottage. It was dark, airless. It hadn't been used since Ollie had gone.

Holding each other, they stumbled into the sofa. Holding each other still, they fell upon it. His tongue licked at her lips, tasting. He pressed light kisses on her throat, her cheeks, her eyelids. Their clothes fell away, and he left long trails of kisses on her shoulders and breasts. She drew him closer, her thighs enfolding him, her hands tightly cupping the back of his head.

'Too long,' he murmured against her mouth.

'Oh, yes,' she whispered. 'Oh, yes, Hank.'

David crouched in the dark, his eyes fixed

on the window. He didn't notice the heavy dew. The flush he had felt rise in his face an hour before had congealed into two seared circles on his cheeks. They stung as if blistered.

'Go on,' Gordon had said carelessly. 'Find a cab and go home.' He hadn't bothered to turn to look at David. He'd kept smiling across the bar at Mandy Sommers, the cocktail waitress.

For the past two months Gordon had insisted on coming to this Georgetown bar because of the tall curvy girl. David admitted that she was good to look at, if you liked her type. And Gordon did.

Her hair was short and curly, framing her face, and very red; not auburn shaded with bronze like Elianne's, or their mother's, but shot through with orange. Her legs were long, encased in black net stockings. Her short flared skirt hit her at mid-thigh. There was something about her smile that David didn't like. A smug knowingness that cut him. Gordon didn't seem to notice that.

Somehow, David didn't know where, Gordon had gotten hold of a couple of fake IDs. The first time they'd tried to use them, David had been scared, although Gordon said it would be okay. As always, Gordon was right. Nobody asked him any questions. Nobody questioned David either. As far as he could tell, nobody had even noticed he was there. It was so easy that Gordon decided to try it again at the end of the same week. That's when Mandy had started playing up to him. When she wasn't busy she'd talk to him. Between customers she'd grin at him. A couple of times, when the place wasn't busy, she grabbed Gordon and got him to dance with her.

David considered her a royal pain in the neck, but Gordon was fascinated. He started leaving big tips. Twenty dollars a night. Fifty dollars another night. He started bringing her small presents.

It didn't matter to David until Gordon told him to grab a cab and go home. Then it began to matter.

But if Gordon hadn't done that, David wouldn't have been staring into the cottage, his teeth chattering and his cheeks burning, and his long legs cramping, as he watched Elianne and Hank.

He watched until he couldn't stand it any more: those movements in the dark; the whispers he couldn't hear. He slid away from the window, moving like a shadow up the long slope to the house. His quick shallow breaths hung in the air before his face. His eyes stung with anger. When he got to his room, he locked the door. He didn't want Gordon to come in. He didn't want to talk to him. He wasn't going to say a word about what he'd seen. It served Gordon right that Hank and Elianne were making love. It served Gordon right.

He took a book from his shelf and methodically tore out every page. Then he sat there and tore each page to shreds.

Finally he went to sleep. He dreamed about Elianne in Hank's arms. He dreamed about Gordon in Mandy's arms.

In the morning, he told Gordon about Hank and Elianne.

Chapter Five

Elianne had managed to keep up with her class work while she was out of school during Keith's illness and the trip to Death Valley with the help of Stacy Gaynor. The two girls became more friendly after that. Stacy was tall and blonde, with a narrow face. She was nineteen, younger than Elianne by three years. But the courses they took together gave them something in common. They exchanged grimaces at the instructors' feeble jokes, and made the same notes of what they had said.

One afternoon, at the end of April, when the two girls had left class together, Elianne discovered that she had a flat tyre, and found the spare flat too. Stacy drove her to Hannah's Gate after no one answered the telephone there.

When they arrived, they found Keith and Hank. The boys had just come in and were still wearing their jackets as they watched a special news programme on television. 'We're leaving Saigon,' Hank said softly, his eyes fixed on the screen, where a helicopter hovered, desperate men clinging to it. 'And we're leaving *them* behind,' he added under his breath.

He looked so sad, pained. As if he too had known the same desperation. Elianne wanted to touch him. Instead, she apologized for interrupting, explaining about the tyres, while Stacy chatted with Keith and looked curiously around the study, eyeing Big Jack's portrait, and the bookcases, and peering out of the window at the long slope of the terraces behind the house.

The next morning Stacy was late to class. She slipped into her seat just as the lecture began. She grinned at Elianne. 'Wait until you hear!'

After class, she picked up as if there'd been no hour's interruption. She said, 'It's the funniest thing, Elianne. I was visiting my grandmother, and looking for things to talk about. You know how you do with old people? So I told her about going to Hannah's Gate with you. And guess what? She knew your grandmother. And your mother and father too.'

'She did? What was her name?'

'Anna Taylor. She's very old now. I mean . . . really old, Elianne. In her seventies at least.'

'Anna Taylor,' Elianne said softly. 'The name's quite familiar. But I don't . . . I'm not sure . . .'

'I'll bet you'd recognize her if you saw her. Anyhow, she's hoping you'll come and visit. I promised I'd ask you. Would you? Visit her, I mean?'

'Of course. I'd be glad to.'

'Today?' Stacy asked.

'Oh, all right. Why not?'

Later, after they'd had lunch together, the girls drove to N Street to see Anna Taylor. Elianne wasn't sure that she'd ever met the older woman before, but plainly she had known Elianne's family, particularly her Grandmother Dora very well. She made much of Elianne, saying what a pretty girl she was. Her mother's daughter all right. That gorgeous auburn hair. The same as Dora's when she was young, the same as Claire's. Most of all Anna Taylor spoke of Dora, and with great affection too, saying. 'She was a fine woman.' and with a sigh, 'She didn't deserve the troubles that were heaped on her. But she bore them with such grace. Even when she was very young. And later too.' She stopped, changed the subject then, leaving Elianne to wonder what she'd been thinking of and hadn't said.

Elianne and Stacy fell into the routine of

weekly visits with the older woman. They'd have tea, and Anna would speak of the past, of parties she had given and gone to. Of her old friends, so many long gone. But always, her conversation came back to Dora and Claire, and to Hannah's Gate.

On one of their visits Stacy's mother was there. She too was tall and blonde. She was as friendly as Stacy, and as out-going. Her husband was with the State Department. They had been stationed abroad for years. Now that they were back in Washington they were just beginning to see old friends again.

It was through Stacy's mother that Elianne was drawn into the same Washington society that her grandmother and mother had known.

She asked Elianne to several dinners. Soon, at Stacy's instigation, she invited Keith and Hank too.

Through her Elianne met people who had known her grandmother, her father and mother. One elderly gentleman told her that he remembered her great-grandfather, Big Jack Gowan, very well, and was disappointed to learn that Elianne had never known him. Another told her that he had worked with her grandfather Casey Loving, at a firm called Geostat, before he went out west, prospecting for oil. Sometimes she was puzzled by comments she heard. The old gentleman who had remembered Big Jack Gowan remarked sadly, 'Unfairly treated, Big Jack. It shouldn't have happened.' Another person said, speaking of Washington during the Second World War, 'And of course, there was Hannah's Gate too. Talked about all over the city. Why, they could all have been murdered in their beds!'

Elianne asked what was meant, but the woman gave her a quick look, said, 'I must get myself a drink,' and hurried off.

Later Elianne remembered those comments. But now they seemed unimportant. They had to do with a past long gone, and had nothing to do with her, with the Hannah's Gate that she knew.

In mid-summer the Gaynors had an evening lawn party. Elianne wore a long pale green shift of chiffon, and bound her hair back with a matching ribbon. She was accompanied by Keith and Hank, both in white flannels and blue blazers.

Pale yellow Japanese lanterns were strung between shiny-leafed holly trees. Long tables covered with white linen were laden with platters of rare roast beef, and others of whole salmon, and fruit arrangements of pineapple and papaya piled high between trays of salad. White-jacketed bartenders carried trays of drinks, wide glasses of champagne, tall Scotches, pale martinis and golden manhattans. A five-piece played continuously.

Stacy took Elianne around to introduce her to several young people. She smiled and talked with them, but at the same time she was thinking of Hannah's Gate. When had there been an affair like this there? Some time, perhaps, but it must have been before she was born. Surely, within her memory, her parents had never entertained. She wondered why. They had the place, the wherewithal. Why had Hannah's Gate always seemed to her a grim prison, where there had been little laughter, rarely music, scarcely joy?

It was as if the old house was afflicted with some unrecognizable blight that soured whatever it touched. She didn't want to believe that, but she sensed the reality of it more and more. She knew that same reality was touching her too. Her and Hank.

She tried not to face what was happening between them but she couldn't ignore it. Since their return from Death Valley, she felt an invisible wall between them. A wall made up of their withheld feelings, their buried memories, their fear and guilt and shame. On her side, it was the three years when she had been away from home. The years about which she never spoke, couldn't ever speak. For him, she wasn't certain. But she remembered his sad and pained face as he watched the American withdrawal from Saigon. Because of that, she thought it must have something to do with his time in Vietnam. But what, she couldn't imagine.

They had built the wall between them in Death Valley, when they behaved as if they had been born that night under the desert stars, with no past and no distant beginnings. And no future too. They had shared nothing but their bodies. In the months since their return they had continued as they had begun.

But now she told herself that Hannah's Gate was spoiling what she had with Hank. And she mustn't allow it to happen. It was then that Hank came to her, drew her into his arms.

She put her doubts aside. She would think about them later. Not now. Smiling at him, she told herself that there was no Hannah's Gate. No dreary memories. No blight. Now there was only Hank. The music was slow and sweet. She pressed close to him, feeling the warmth of his body. Oh, it was good to belong to him. Good to pretend that this dance, this evening, would never end.

But slowly, insistently, she became aware of a tall heavy woman who stared at her from the edge of the dance floor. No matter which way she turned within the circle of Hank's arms, Elianne felt those eyes follow her.

Elianne didn't recognize the woman. She

didn't think she'd ever seen her before. But she felt as if she ought to. There was an intensity in the woman's thick body, in her forward thrust white head.

Although the air was warm, Elianne suddenly shivered.

'What?' Hank asked.

'I don't know. Just a feeling . . .'

He smiled, and tightened his arm at her waist.

Carrie Day gave the young couple one last look, and turned away. So that was Elianne Merrill. Dora's granddaughter. Claire's daughter. Elianne. The present mistress of Hannah's Gate.

Carrie hadn't seen Elianne for years. There had been a time when the older woman had been drawn back to the Cleveland Park house, had driven to Honey Locust Lane in her old Volkswagen and parked there, watching the place where she had once lived. She'd seen Claire then, and Elianne, and the two small boys. She'd seen Leigh Merrill, too. They hadn't known she was there, hadn't sensed her staring.

'You're nothing to me,' Dora Gowan had said. Dora Gowan Loving. 'You're nothing to me.' But Carrie knew better. No matter what Dora wanted to pretend to believe, Carrie was her younger half-sister, the unacknowledged daughter of Dora's father, Big Jack Gowan, and his secretary and mistress and love of his life, Betsey Ferguson, Carrie's mother. That made Carrie a great-aunt, or at least half a great-aunt to Elianne. But Elianne owned Hannah's Gate, and Carrie had nothing.

The older woman pictured the big house as she had last seen it. The brick walls, the iron gate, the bronze sign emblazoned with its name. How grand it had become. How grand Leigh Merrill's vision had been. And how lucky he'd inherited his uncle's fortune.

To Carrie, the place remained the same as when she had first seen it, when she had lived in the third-floor attic room, her small typewriter set on a child's desk, the same typewriter she still used. The shelves for envelopes and papers. The cardboard files for her short stories. Oh, she'd had dreams then. Dreams about Hannah's Gate, and having her share of it. And dreams about her writing too. She'd thought to see her name in the *Atlantic Monthly*, the *New Yorker*. Instead she'd seen her articles, unsigned, in *People* magazine, more lately in the *National Enquirer*. She'd been so busy earning a living, surviving, that there'd been no time for the short stories that she'd hoped to write. Now, after all these years, she was a fixture in Washington. She was still earning her living, doing freelance articles for whoever would buy them, still feeding gossip and small bits of information to whoever would pay for it.

She looked back now on her life at Hannah's Gate as the good time. The time when she had dreams. Margo Desales had died then, and Linda Grant, and Logan Jessup too. But she'd had her room at the top of the house, her own small world. Until Dora Loving forced her into exile, and left what should have been Carrie's to Claire. The bad luck of the house had touched Claire too, and all the others. Rea. Ian. Leigh. And now Elianne owned Hannah's Gate.

Over Hank's shoulder Elianne met Carrie Day's eyes, an unblinking expressionless gaze. Cold touched Elianne, and once again she pressed closer to Hank.

But the music came to an end. They stepped apart. Hank said, 'I'll go and see how Keith is. He's alone now.'

For a good part of the evening Stacy had been with Keith. Hank and Elianne had been glad to see that. At Hannah's Gate, she was always attentive to him, and he seemed to like her. But now she had drifted off to talk to someone else.

Elianne intended to go with Hank, but Garet Morley asked her for the next dance. She had met him earlier. Although he was in his late forties, and had a touch of grey at his temples, he gave the impression of being a much younger man. He was a senator from a middle-western state, a much sought after bachelor.

Carrie Day saw him lead Elianne on to the dance floor as the music began again. She stood stock still, her eyes narrowed. Her hand slipped slowly into the big bag she carried, and her fingers closed around her camera.

Garet Morley said, 'I've been watching you all evening.'

Elianne smiled at him, but didn't speak. She wasn't used to small talk. It was easier to be silent than to talk about the weather or what was happening in Washington. She didn't suppose he'd care to discuss the Romans in England, which was what she'd been reading about this week for her class in ancient history.

Garet went on, 'It surprises me that I've never met you before. I've heard about your family, of course. Especially about your great-grandfather.'

'That's what comes of staying in the city where your family has lived for a long time,' she said.

'And it doesn't happen that often these days, does it?' He smiled down at her. 'There are advantages. And, of course, disadvantages.'

She was thinking largely of the disadvantages. What did it matter who her great-grandfather had been. Or her grandfather? Or her parents? Why did people care about her lineage, as if she were a prize bull? What did people expect of her, or want of her? It didn't matter to her that she was a Merrill, out of a Loving, out of a Gowan. Why should it matter to anyone else?

The music quickened. Garet's hold on her tightened. A breeze swept across the lawn, sent the shadows of the trees dancing, and the yellow Japanese lanterns swaying.

'I hope I haven't offended you,' he said.

'You haven't. Why would you think so?'

He laughed. 'You have a very open face, Elianne. More than open — eloquent. You were annoyed by my chitchat about your family. And it showed.'

Courtesy required a denial, and she was about to say the words when she heard a sharp outcry. A shout of fear. The music stopped with a discordant jangle. The warm air was inexplicably shot through with chill.

Elianne jerked to a stop within the circle of Garet's arms, and heard him swear under his breath.

Nearby, so close that she could almost reach out and touch him, stood a man wearing a nylon stocking over his face. The blurring of his features made him look like a character from a horror movie. And then she saw behind him three other masked men. All had guns in their hands. One wore a waiter's uniform. The others had on blue jeans, black wind-breakers and black boots.

Garet's tall body stiffened. His arms fell away from her.

'Everybody be still,' the man closest to them yelled, his faceless head slowly turning to watch the group. 'Don't move. Don't try anything. This is a hold up.' As he spoke his gun moved in a slow menacing arc.

The other masked men imitated the movement, so that four guns, glinting in the light of the yellow lanterns, seemed to point in turn at each of the frozen guests, while the lacy shadows of the trees drifted across their blood-less faces.

A thin wail of terror spiralled into the silence. A glass fell, shattered with the tinkle of distant music.

'Men, drop your wallets! Women, drop your bags and jewellery! Now!'

There were small sounds. Rustles. Movements. Mumbles. The assembly followed the shouted orders. Wallets fell to the wooden slats of the dance floor with a thud or soundlessly on the close-cropped grass. Jewellery made sparkling paths through the dim light as it fell from trembling fingers.

The guns within the steady hands seemed as large as cannon. The men carrying canvas bags were swift as dancers, gliding through the pale yellow light.

'Hurry! Hurry!'

Elianne took off her emerald earrings. She dropped them into the bag held out to her. The man who held it was so close she could feel his body warmth, smell his sweat.

'Oh, no!' a woman cried. 'Not my wedding ring!'

Elianne felt rather than saw Garet's swift lunge. There was a thud, a yelp.

Two shots exploded into the frozen air. Spits of fire. One. Then another.

Garet! His heavy weight sagged into Elianne, then dropped away as he fell at her feet. There was blood on his white jacket. A frightening greyness bleached his face. She knelt beside him, aware of the swift withdrawal of the gunmen. Aware of the rising tide of screams, sobs, oaths.

She leaned over Garet, whispering, 'Don't move now,' while she caught the end of his jacket, pulled it up and wadded it to press against the wound in his chest.

Hank raced for the house to telephone for help.

Elianne was hardly aware of the chaos around her. She leaned over Garet. He opened his eyes. 'Is it bad?' he asked.

'I don't think so,' she said. With a steady hand she continued to press the wadded end of the jacket against the red stain blooming on his shirt front, feeling the hot wet slick of his blood as it oozed between her fingers. Time passed in quick bursts, but she wasn't aware of that either. She was so intent on Garet Morley that she didn't even notice the flash-bulb of a camera.

It flared, faded, flared again, faded.

Carrie Day slipped the camera into her bag, already considering the lead paragraph for the story she would write, already thinking about the Gowans, the Lovings, the Merrills, and the tragedies of Hannah's Gate. Slowly, talking to no one, she made her way through the confusion, while sirens screamed in the street before the house.

Gordon's face was flushed. His eyes glittered under narrowed lids. He offered the newspaper to Elianne. 'You're a heroine,' he said. 'You should be proud of yourself.'

She shuddered when she looked. Familiar features, twisted with terror. Long hair like curtains around her cheeks. A spray of blood on the pale gown. She was kneeling beside Garet Morley, both her hands pressed to his chest, a darkness spreading between her fingers. Garet's face was in shadow. In the background there were faint silhouettes of ladies' gowns, men's feet.

Now she remembered those strange flashes of light that she had registered but not identified. Now she understood that they'd been camera flashes. Who had taken these pictures at the moment that Garet fell?

'Read the story,' Gordon said. 'You ought to be interested. It's because you had to be such a heroine that it's all in there!'

She pushed the paper away. She didn't want to read about what had happened. Plainly the bandits hadn't been caught. If they had been, the headline would have said so. There had been so much confusion. The ambulance had taken Garet away. The police hadn't allowed her to go with him. She wondered how he was. If he would be all right.

'Read it,' Gordon insisted. 'And then see what it says on page A5.'

'Leave her alone, Gordon.' It was Hank, pushing Keith's wheel chair, into the room.

Gordon ignored Hank. He went on, his voice thin with sarcasm. 'It must have been a damn fine party. All the VIPs in town. Do you suppose the Gaynors set up the robbery so they could make the front pages?'

Keith smiled and said gently, 'Gordon, you know what? You're being impossible. Nobody could have helped what happened. Stop accusing Elianne.'

'What do you care?' Gordon demanded. 'It's nothing to you. It's not your name spread all over the papers. You're a Devlin. Nobody's going to write stories about you.'

'All true,' Keith retorted. 'But who cares what they write?'

'It's enough to make a man puke,' Gordon said. 'He picks up the morning paper, and there, right in front of him, on the first page, there's a picture of his sister looking like a witch. With blood on her hands and clothes. And you turn a few pages, and right in front of you is your own name: Merrill. And that's not all. Merrill. Hannah's Gate. Grandpa and Grandma Loving. All the way back to our great-grandfather . . . the honourable, the wonderful and extraordinary Big Jack Gowan, of Mississippi, Washington and Cleveland Park.'

He was mocking the memory of Dora now, stories of the past she had known. She hadn't recounted the accusations against her father . . . the tales that he'd accepted money to vote for certain bills . . . the disgrace and resignation that had followed. Gordon was sneering at his memories of her hopes for him. He didn't care about her hopes. He was content to be his father's son, a Merrill of Hannah's

101

Gate. And he didn't want to see his name, his father's name, in the daily newspaper.

Later, when Elianne read the articles about the robbery at the Gaynors', she was shocked to see how much space was devoted to her and to Hannah's Gate. They went all the way back to long before she was born. Back to the 1940s in Washington, and the war. Back to Big Jack's loss of his Senate seat. They told of Casey Loving's death in Chicago, and Ian Loving's death in Santa Fe, and Rea Loving's death in Mexico. They spoke of the two murders at Hannah's Gate, describing Margo Desales and Linda Grant as friends of the family, and Logan Jessup as a German spy. They expanded at length on the fact that Leigh had inherited the fortune left by his uncle, Jeremiah Merrill, a friend of the deceased President Roosevelt. They didn't mention the details of Jeremiah's death, for all knowledge of those died with Leigh and were never known thereafter. But Dora's death, and Claire's, and Leigh's were all mentioned as part of the long-term history of Hannah's Gate, part of its bad luck history. The Gowans, the Lovings, the Merrills . . . star struck, the paper said.

Elianne read the words over and over again, and then flung the paper away from her. She didn't believe it! It wasn't true! How could it be? She remembered that her Grandmother Dora had often reminisced about meeting Casey Loving after World War I, and how he had looked in his uniform, and how she'd fallen in love with him at first sight. And always, Elianne recalled, when she finished that tale, she'd look around the room, perplexed, bewildered, as if she'd lost something and didn't know where. And her Grandmother Dora had spoken of the depression and how she'd managed to hang on to Hannah's Gate, and of Jeremiah Merrill who had loved Leigh so much he'd left everything he had to him. Grandmother Dora had never mentioned anything scary, never said there'd been murders here. Once more Elianne told herself that she didn't believe it.

And now, while Gordon glared at her, she said, 'I'm going to call the hospital, find out how Garet is.'

'I don't understand,' Hank said softly. 'The robbery was at the Gaynors, after all. Senator Morley was shot. I wonder why there's so much written about Hannah's Gate. It doesn't really have a thing to do with what happened.'

Nobody answered him.

Elianne heard again the flat sound of the two shots, felt Garet's weight sag against her . . . the tumult that followed . . . the four men disappearing.

Within instants, it seemed, the garden had swarmed with policemen. The ambulance pulled away. The officers moved quietly, quickly, from one guest to another. They took down descriptions. The man who had spoken. The faint accent, identified by some as Spanish perhaps. The descriptions of the men. Slight. Dark. In jeans and windbreakers, except for the one who wore a waiter's uniform. Names and addresses were collected. Gradually the guests were allowed to depart.

When Elianne, accompanied by Hank and Keith, returned home, she found Gordon and David waiting. They had heard news flashes on late night television, and had seen a few dark shots of the Gaynor house surrounded by police cars. From the morning papers, they had garnered the rest of the details.

Now Gordon said, 'They claim the robbers were Puerto Rican.' He looked hard at Hank.

'Probably,' Hank said. 'Judging by their accents . . .'

'Puerto Rican.' Elianne remembered reading about the bombing of Fraunces Tavern in New York. It had been said then that Puerto Rican nationalists were responsible.

'And you ought to know, Hank.' Gordon said thoughtfully. He was obliquely referring to the fact that Hank's father had been Puerto Rican, though his mother had been American.

Hank was unperturbed by Gordon's suggestive tone. 'There is a small group that wants independence from us.' By 'us', Hank meant the United States; he also meant himself. He was letting Gordon know that he had understood the hint. He was telling Gordon that he considered himself an American.

Elianne excused herself. She called the hospital, and learned that Garet Morley was off the critical list now. She ordered flowers sent to him. When he was well enough for visitors, she would go to see him, she decided.

Late that same afternoon three FBI agents came to the house. They went over the same ground covered the night before by the police. Elianne had nothing to add to what she had already said. She had been dropping her earrings into the canvas bag. Garet had lunged forward. The robber had fired twice, and Garet had fallen against her, and then collapsed. She didn't recognize the masked men. She doubted that she would be able to identify them. When the agents departed, she assumed that she would never see them again. But at the beginning of the following week they were back.

This time they closeted themselves with Hank. They wanted to know about him, about his connection to Puerto Rico. There was, and never had been, a connection. His father had been Puerto Rican, his mother American. They had lived at Big Sur, in California, but had died in the mud slide years ago. They talked a little longer, mentioning his two years in Vietnam, asking him about what he had done since then. But it was plain to him that they already knew everything there was to know about him. Evidently they had checked his military file and background before coming to talk to him. They didn't mention Bien Kok, but he guessed they knew about that too.

He supposed that it was his name, Ramos, or perhaps his appearance, that had led them to check him out. Plainly they believed that Puerto Rican terrorists had robbed the party at the Gaynor house. Hank didn't know that their attention had been particularly directed to him by their receipt of an anonymous letter which accused him of masterminding the robbery.

It was the only real lead the agents had. When that proved false their investigation came to a dead end. The men who had invaded the Gaynor home disappeared into the world from which they had emerged, and were never apprehended.

The Yenching Palace was Gordon's favourite Chinese restaurant. He took David there on Friday night. They shared a huge bowl of hot and sour soup, shrimp toast and steamed dumplings, an order of Peking duck and another of moshu pork.

They finished the meal with tea and fortune cookies.

David's read, *You will do great things.*

You will have all that you dream of, said Gordon's.

David's wide and unblinking eyes searched Gordon's face. Gordon looked back at him, and laughed.

Chapter Six

Jake Babbitt squinted into the golden June sunlight. 'My love is divine,' he said aloud. Then he sighed. Lately he had taken no comfort in the words. Something was happening. He didn't know what.

As he drove through Ranchos, he finished the orange he was eating. He dropped the peels on to the three-day-old Albuquerque *Journal*, and threw the messy package out of the van window. He saw a headline about the Bicentennial celebration, but didn't read the accompanying story. He didn't notice the grainy picture of Elianne, kneeling beside Garet Morely, nor the column next to it that described the robbery in which the senator had been shot, so he didn't notice the run-on on page A5 that told about her and her family, and Hannah's Gate.

Three months later there was a story in a magazine carried by a shop on the plaza in

Taos. It had the the same picture of Elianne kneeling beside Morley. It also had several other photographs of her with him. One was taken when he was her escort at a charity ball, where each ticket was a one-thousand-dollar contribution. Another was of the two of them strolling along the C & O Canal tow path not far from Fletcher's Landing. A third showed him entering Hannah's Gate, carrying a huge bouquet of flowers.

The text of the story was about the rumoured romance, an April-December affair, between a senator and the heiress of a tragedy-struck family. Once again the history of the Gowans, the Lovings and the Merrills was described in intimate detail.

Jake didn't see that either.

Mandy Sommers had read most of the newspaper articles that followed the shooting of Garet Morley. Not that she was interested in current events, or Puerto Rican terrorists. But she *was* interested in what happened at Hannah's Gate. Hannah's Gate. In Cleveland Park. She remembered the night that Gordie had told her about the place.

She'd said, during a lull, when there was time to stand and talk a minute, 'You must live around here. Otherwise you wouldn't be in so often.'

'Not far away. In Cleveland Park.'

'Cleveland Park. Lucky you. That *is* nice.'

'At Hannah's Gate,' he said, smiling. 'That's the name of my place.'

'Think of that,' Mandy said. 'Hannah's Gate.' She made it sound as if she knew what he was talking about. It could have been a dog house as far as she was concerned. But she knew what Gordie wanted. She'd learned a long time before how to read a man's mind. And he wasn't a man, no matter what he thought. He was a boy. Maybe he'd always be a boy. Not that she would tell him that, or treat him that way. She knew what she was doing. She saw how much money he spent. Hannah's Gate. It had a good rich sound to it, even if she'd never heard of it before. It had the ring of jewellery, and cars, and mink coats. So, when the stories began to appear, she read them with growing interest. There was more there than she'd imagined. Not that she cared about a crooked congressman out of olden times, or a couple of murders that had taken place when she was a baby. It was what Gordie had that interested her. She was determined to get some of it for herself. And she knew how to do it — through him.

Thus, when Gordon and David came into the bar on a cold November night, she gave Gordon a warm smile, wriggled her narrow hips at him, and pretended David wasn't there.

But David was very much there, quiet as always, sullen, his hazel eyes narrowed but missing nothing.

This wasn't a place he liked. It was Gordon's favourite. So, of course, that's where the two of them went. There were many others in Georgetown. Walk either way, on both sides of M Street, and lights blinked and beckoned. Music spilled out through open doors, swirling over the crowded pavements and across the fleets of cars and trucks that filled the road. The air was laced with the hot burned odour of car exhausts, and thickened with the smell of scorched grease, and occasionally a gust of sweetness: chocolate and caramelized sugar.

Gordon always wanted to come here because of Mandy.

He settled at the bar. David sat beside him. In a little while their orders were put before them. David picked up his glass, allowing the whisky and ice to touch his lips before wiping the harsh taste away with the back of his hand. He hated the stuff. But if you sat at the bar you had to have something in front of you.

Mandy slid a big smile at Gordon as she passed by.

Gordon grinned and raised his glass in a silent toast. 'Hey! Mandy! Come and talk to me.'

Something cold and hard settled in David's chest.

'In a minute,' she said. 'When things quiet down.' She went on, into the back room.

Gordon turned to David, 'Nice, isn't she?'

David shrugged. He knew what was coming. It had happened before.

Gordon frowned, 'Look, if you don't want to stay, you don't have to.'

'Is that what you want? For me to go?'

'Not now.' Gordon hesitated. 'I mean not right away. But maybe . . . a little later . . . And I guess this is boring for you.'

'We always used to stick together,' David said sulkily. 'You said it would be that way forever. We're brothers. Just the two of us. Against . . . against . . .' His voice faded.

'That hasn't changed,' Gordon told him. 'What makes you think it has?'

'You,' David said. 'You've changed.'

Gordon laughed. 'No. You're wrong. I'm just doing what comes naturally.'

'I don't know what you mean.'

'Sure you do. I've told you about it. And one of these days it'll be the same for you.'

'It won't be,' David said. 'I don't need anybody but you.'

Gordon smiled at him. 'Wait and see.'

The cold hard something in David's chest dissolved. 'All right,' he said. 'But don't forget. It's us, just the two of us.' He got to his feet. 'And now I guess I'll go home.'

Gordon didn't ask him to stay for a while. He ordered another drink and settled back to watch Mandy come and go.

It had been several months since he wandered into the place and saw her: Mandy Sommers. She said she was thirty-one. He guessed she was maybe thirty-five. She made a big thing out of her age, saying that when she was with him she felt as if she were robbing the cradle. When she said 'with him' she meant talking to him over the bar. So far she hadn't even let him take her home after work. The only time he'd been alone with her was in the bar, after hours, when the bartender went out back to the storeroom to do some late at night inventory. He'd had time to kiss her then, but no more than that. He knew that one of these nights it would be different. She could joke all she wanted to about robbing the cradle, it didn't make any difference to him. She could be old, really old. He still wanted her. The way she was now. He didn't care how long she'd been that way.

Mandy got behind the bar. She served other customers, made small talk with them, but winked at Gordon when she went by.

He finished his drink, ordered another. She brought it to him, then lingered, to polish the scarred wood with a dirty rag. He tried to think of something to say, but couldn't. His mind was empty except for a picture. He, with Mandy in his arms, holding her tight against him . . .

'Where's your brother?' she asked.

'He went home, I guess.'

She smiled into Gordon's eyes. 'Then you're on your own for once.'

'Yes. I'm on my own, Mandy.'

'Want to take me home?'

'Sure,' he told her. 'Why not?' Being cool. She didn't have to know how anxious he was. But he looked eagerly at his watch. Almost midnight. Only a couple of hours to go.

She saw that, and laughed, and hurried away to serve someone else.

Later, when she'd returned to the bar, she asked, 'Everything quiet at your place now?'

'At Hannah's Gate? Yes. Sure. It's all over.' *My* place, he was thinking. My home. *Mine.* By rights, it should have been. He was the oldest son. He should have had it. That was what his father intended. He knew it was. But his mother . . . oh, damn her . . . it wasn't fair.

Down at the end of the bar, but close enough to hear, a man sat alone, listening, although he pretended not to be. His name was Carl Utah. As soon as Hannah's Gate was mentioned his ears pricked. He finished his beer, set down the glass, then slid closer, past four stools, to seat himself next to Gordon. As an excuse for the move, he asked Mandy for another beer. Then he turned to Gordon and asked for a match.

Gordon obliged, his attention fixed on Mandy.

She was saying, 'I'd love to see your place some time. I mean, after what I've read . . . it sounds so exciting. You know, Gordie . . . knowing it's your home.'

Carl Utah listened. He was a big man, with large gnarled hands. His eyes were a deep soft brown, and his longish hair was brown too, but sun-faded. So this plump young man was Gordon Merrill, he thought. Gordon Merrill, who must be Casey Loving's grandson, if Carl had worked it out correctly. And he was sure he had. He'd read all the stories about Hannah's Gate too, so it was easy to figure out. Casey Loving had had a wife named Dora, in Washington. A wife, a son, and two daughters. The son and one daughter had died young. The other daughter, Claire, had had two sons, David and Gordon, and a daughter, Elianne. Carl wondered about David and Elianne now. What they were like. His eyes slid sideways to study Gordon, as he listened.

'Yes,' Mandy was saying. 'One of these days I've just got to see Hannah's Gate, Gordie.'

And Gordon answered, 'Sure. One of these days you will.'

Carl drank his beer, and smoked his cigarette. He decided that one of these days he, too, was going to Hannah's Gate.

There was an error in the story Carrie Day had written about Garet Morley and Elianne. It was true that Garet visited Hannah's Gate, bringing flowers. It was also true that he had taken Elianne to the charity ball, and walked with her on the tow path near the C & O Canal. But the suggestion that theirs was an April-December romance was false.

Since Garet's recovery, he and Elianne had become friends. If, in the beginning, he had any romantic feelings for her, he soon knew that she loved Hank Ramos. Not that she ever told him so. Nor had she ever done anything in his presence to reveal her feelings. It was just that Garet liked her, and was a man of some experience. Having seen them together many times, he understood.

Elianne accepted his frequent invitations because she enjoyed his company, but also because it was just as well for David and Gordon to believe she was interested in Garet rather than in Hank. She didn't realize that they were in no way deceived.

Then, in early December, Garet invited

Elianne to attend an informal holiday dinner at the White House. It was an experience not many people had, and she, along with Stacy, shopped for days before they found a dress at Garfinkle's that seemed suitable. It was a dark green brocade, with a high narrow waist set with a wide dark green velvet bow. It had a high neck with a tiny mandarin collar, and elbow-length sleeves. She wore her hair pulled back and high, and tied it in a ribbon of the same colour.

When Garet came to pick her up, he said, smiling. 'You're going to be the prettiest girl in the room.'

But Elianne's eyes went to Hank. It was his approval she hoped for. 'Have a good time,' he said softly. 'Remember everything so you can tell me about it when you get home.'

It was exciting to drive to the White House in Garet's limousine, to enter between the tall iron gates and pass beneath the brilliantly-lit chandelier that hung over the north portico.

The President and Mrs Ford had invited nine couples. After an hour of socializing, having drinks and canapes, they were seated in groups of six at three round tables.

The Blue Room was oval-shaped. Its walls were covered with pale blue damask shot through with gold threads, its windows draped with the same fabric. As always, there were yellow flowers on the white mantel over the large fireplace, and on corner stands.

The President was a good host, relaxed and smiling. He gave no sign that he was just finishing up his term, and that a new President would be moving into the White House on January 20th. Mrs Ford was friendly, moving with a dancer's grace among her guests.

But during the cocktail hour Elianne became uncomfortably aware of the hard cold gaze of an older woman across the room. She was tall and wide-shouldered. Long dark hair was swept back from her face into a thick chignon. Her narrowed dark eyes were heavily mascaraed, her lips a scarlet slash. She looked vaguely familiar to Elianne. There was, then, no opportunity to ask Garet about her.

Later Elianne found herself and Garet seated at the same table as the older woman and her escort. Elianne wished that there had been time to enquire of Garet who she was. For the woman continued to stare at her, barely acknowledging the introductions made by her escort.

When Elianne learned that her name was Stella Corless, she was even more mystified. Elianne had never before met the still famous, only recently retired, movie star. She didn't know the woman's escort either.

Soon, though, Elianne began to understand that the woman had known Garet before, for the actress smiled sweetly at him, and said, 'Long time no see, my old friend.'

'Yes. It has been a while, Stella,' Garet replied.

'And you're completely recovered from your . . . what would you call it? Accident? Assassination attempt?' Stella's laugh was not pleasant.

'I'm recovered,' Garet said. He turned to Elianne, plainly intending to end the interrogation. 'Did you have a few words with Mrs Ford? She's an interesting woman, isn't she?'

Elianne had no time to reply.

Stella said loudly, 'I hope you weren't shot in the groin, Garet. By the looks of your date, you'll need whatever power you can work up.' And then, smiling with false sweetness, Stella turned her attention to Elianne, 'Your first time at the White House, isn't it dear?'

'Yes. It is, Mrs Corless,' Elianne answered.

'Ms Corless,' the woman said. Then: 'Yes, I thought it must be your first visit. You have that wide-eyed stupid look that tourists always have.'

'Stella,' Garet said firmly. 'That's enough, isn't it?'

'Oh?' She turned shining eyes on him. 'You don't agree?'

Elianne realized then that the woman was either drunk or drugged. It could be nothing else. The shining eyes. The loud voice. The failure of good manners.

Another of the guests spoke. Someone answered. The conversation became general. White-gloved waiters served the food. Wine was poured.

Elianne began to enjoy the talk of politics, the favourite topic of conversation in Washington, at the White House, as well as in every restaurant and bar.

Then Stella leaned back in her chair, looking directly at Elianne. 'What a lucky thing for you that Garet was shot just at your feet.'

A silence fell across the table.

Elianne wondered how best to deal with such a woman. In those long ago years when she had been with people affected by drugs, she had learned to ignore them. If she couldn't ignore them, she knew enough to get out of their way.

But Stella Corless was different. It was impossible to ignore her. She didn't permit it. Yet Elianne couldn't rise to her level of insult. She hadn't the faintest idea of where, or how, to begin. And she couldn't get up and walk away either.

Garet was saying, 'It was much luckier for me than for Elianne. She probably kept me from bleeding to death.'

Stella laughed. 'Oh, my dear, so dramatic. But of course, it would have been such a great loss . . . to the ladies, and to the party as well.'

Once again one of the other guests spoke hastily. Another answered. The waiters brought coffee, then brandy.

Elianne refused the brandy, accepted the coffee.

Stella refused the coffee, accepted the brandy. When she had warmed the balloon glass in her long slender hands, then sipped daintily at it, she said, 'This is a wonderful country, isn't it, Elianne? A small nothing like you at the White House . . . I do hope you appreciate what Garet has done for you.'

Garet rose, drawing Elianne with him, 'Come, Elianne,' he said. 'I'm sure the others will excuse us. There's someone I want you to meet.'

She went with him, her cheeks burning. It had been a painful experience to be at the centre of attention, to have been made the butt of Stella Corless' jealous anger. For now Elianne could see that was what had been at the bottom of it.

When Garet spoke, he confirmed Elianne's impressions. 'We were friends a long time ago,' he said. 'Now I can't imagine what I thought I saw in her.'

'She's still a very attractive woman.'

'No, she isn't,' Garet answered. 'She proved that tonight. I'm sorry, Elianne. I didn't intend to expose you to that.'

Elianne watched as Stella Corless walked slowly to the door, leaning heavily on her escort's arm. There, turning to smile at those behind her, she suddenly staggered. Her escort held her on her feet and hurried her out, without pausing to say goodnight to the President and Mrs Ford.

'She's drunk,' Garet said disgustedly.

Elianne didn't answer. She wanted to forget Stella Corless, never to hear her name or to think of her again.

But two days later, in a column in the Washington *Post*, there was a complete description of the incident. It went on to state that unfortunately Stella Corless hadn't realized that she was talking to the heiress to the fortune of Jeremiah Merrill, a confidant of President Franklin D. Roosevelt, as well as the heiress to Hannah's Gate, her family's long-time Washington home, and that she was great-granddaughter of Senator Big Jack Gowan. Hannah's Gate, and the Gowan, Loving, and Merrill families were notable, the article went on to say, for the number of tragedies associated with them.

★ ★ ★

That article, or parts of it, was printed in several other publications. It was the mention in *People* magazine, with a picture of Elianne alongside it, that Jake Babbitt read.

The photograph was a clear one. Elianne had a faint smile on her lips, and her eyes were looking straight into the camera.

He saw that his Ella Em was Elianne Merrill. She lived in a place called Hannah's Gate, in Washington, D.C.

He hadn't seen her in more than five years, but he'd never forgotten her.

He reached into his pocket and took out what was there. Four crumpled bills, a quarter, a nickle, two pennies. He smiled wryly. It wasn't much. But it would do. He'd travelled on less before.

Mandy Sommers read *People* magazine regularly. She saw Elianne's picture, and read the accompanying story. That night, when Gordon came into the bar, she showed it to him, and to David, who was with him.

With David peering over his shoulder, Gordon read it. A flush rose in his cheeks. His eyes glittered. 'Damn her!'

David stared at the spray of Christmas holly tacked over the bar. What was Mandy up to? 'It's a good picture of your sister, isn't it?'

123

Mandy said brightly. And: 'When are you going to introduce me to her, Gordie?'

David's eyes moved from her face to Gordon's, then back.

'One of these days,' Gordon said. 'When the time's right.'

'And when's the time going to be right?'

'I told you. One of these days.'

'All I've heard about Hannah's Gate . . .' she murmured. A customer at the end of the bar called her name. She flashed a smile at Gordon, moved away.

David sagged in his seat. Too bad that she had been interrupted. Gordon hated to be pushed. He hated to be told what to do. If she'd kept on at him, maybe he'd have gotten mad. David was very anxious for Gordon to get good and mad at Mandy.

Carl Utah, sitting close by, shifted his chair closer to Gordon. They'd been exchanging greetings, having small conversations, for some time now. Carl wanted to keep that going. He said, 'I guess Hannah's Gate is a pretty big place.'

'It is,' Gordon said.

'Lots of ground too?' Carl already knew the answer. He'd been out to Cleveland Park and Honey Locust Lane. He'd seen the house, the tall magnolia trees, the brick wall that enclosed the terraced garden and pool and cottage. He'd

124

ambled around the outside and looked at it from every angle, all the while remembering the small house he'd grown up in in the tiny New Mexican town, remembering the geraniums in tin cans and the cactus garden near the front steps.

Gordon nodded absently to Carl's question. He was busy thinking about later on. Maybe Mandy would let him go home with her. It was hard to tell. A week or more, ten days to be exact, had passed since she'd last said, 'Okay, Gordie. If you want to.' And she laughed. 'But I always feel so silly. I mean, robbing the cradle.' When she didn't take him home with her, he guessed she took someone else. It made him mad, but he couldn't do anything about that. At least not yet. His eyes slid towards David. If this was going to be the night, he'd have to get rid of him somehow.

Now Carl said, 'The job I've been on, at the gas station . . . it looks like it's going to fade out.'

'Is that right?'

Carl shrugged. 'I'll get something else. I'm not worried. There's jobs around. Construction, maybe. Or gardening.' Carl knew how to do a lot of things. He'd been taking care of himself since his mother died when he was in high school. There had only been the two

of them for most of his life. He hardly remembered his father. Carl knew he'd been
around for a while. Then, suddenly, when Carl
was four or five, the tall dark-haired man had
gone away and never come back. His mother
had said he'd gone to Washington, D.C. Later,
when Carl was older, she'd said he died. That
was the end of his having a real family. But
before she died, Maria told him that she didn't
want him to feel alone in this world. He had
to know about his Washington family, and
Hannah's Gate. It hadn't seemed real to him
until he'd sat at the bar and heard Gordon
talk about Hannah's Gate. And then Carl had
read about it, and the three families it belonged
to. He read about the murders that had taken
place there, and then he read about the death
of Casey Loving in Chicago. It amused him
that so much was known about the Gowans,
the Lovings and the Merrills. Yet there was
much that wasn't known. He, Carl Utah, was
the proof of that. It amused him that he himself was the secret. And it made him curious
too. Why had it happened? How come his father had called himself Utah, and lived part-
time in New Mexico? How come he'd been
born Utah, instead of Loving?

He said to Gordon. 'Maybe you've got
something for me to do at your place. I'm
a pretty good handyman, if I say so myself.

126

And I've got a green thumb that doesn't quit.'

'I don't know,' Gordon answered. 'Let me think about it.' He turned to David, who was shifting restlessly. 'What's the matter?'

'Nothing,' David told him, looking down at his beer. His glass was still full. He hated beer. It made his stomach burn and his ears ring. He was never comfortable sitting at the bar. Even with the fake I.D. in his pocket, he felt guilty. He didn't know what he'd say if somebody came up and challenged him. It never seemed to bother Gordon that any old time they could be thrown out, maybe even be put in jail for being there.

David would much rather have been out of doors, wandering around in the streets. There was plenty to look at. The Hare Krishnas in their saffron robes, the men's heads shaved, ringing bells, the women in swirling skirts and floating tops and veils adrift along their shoulders, swatting tambourines, and swooping down with smiles and laughter. Trumpeters on the corners, thrusting their horns at the sky, with mats at their feet for donations. Guitar players, gaunt-faced and soulful, strumming music from faraway hills. Motorcyclists, with thick tattooed arms, wearing red sweat rags to hold back their long hair. The smells of pizza, popcorn, and souvlaki . . . There was a lot to do in Georgetown beside sit in

127

the bar and wait for Mandy Sommers to pay attention to Gordon.

David took a deep breath and said, 'Why don't we go out and walk around for a while?'

'Why don't you go, David? I'll be here. You can come back later.'

That, David told himself, was just what he was not going to do.

'Or, if you want to, you can go on home.'

'No. I'm not going to walk around, and I'm not going home.' David answered. 'I'm going to stay here.' But only a little later, he went out into the street. He ambled slowly down the block, and then he caught a cab and went back to Hannah's Gate.

Gordon came down to breakfast earlier than usual, holding in his hand the *People* magazine that Mandy had given him.

He poured a glass of orange juice for himself, prepared a bowl of dry cereal, filled a mug with coffee. He didn't greet, nor even look at Keith and Hank and Elianne, who were already at the table. But, before he sat down, he dropped the magazine in front of Elianne, saying, 'I guess you'll want to see this. You seem to glory in making a fool of yourself, and dragging all our names in the mud.'

'What's the matter?' Keith asked.

Elianne gave the picture and the accompa-

128

nying story a quick glance. Colour flooded into her face. She remembered Stella Corless' stinging voice. She didn't need to read again about her visit to the White House. Every moment there was painfully stamped into her memory, even though she wanted to forget it, to pretend it had never happened.

'More of the same,' Gordon said disdainfully. 'Elianne never learns. Every time she goes out with Garet Morley she ends up in the newspapers.' Gordon snorted. 'Maybe that's why she does it.'

'Oh, leave it alone,' Keith told him disgustedly. 'It's not her fault. Why are you blaming her?' When Elianne offered him the magazine, he shook his head. 'I don't want to read it.' And then: 'Don't pay any attention to what they say.'

'But why does it keep happening? Who does it? Why should anybody care about me?'

'The papers think people will be interested,' Hank told her.

'But I'm not important,' she said heatedly. 'Stella Corless called me a nobody, and she was right. I *am* a nobody. And that's all I want to be.'

'But you're not,' Gordon said softly. 'Every time they write about you it proves that you're not a nobody. We're Merrills. We live in Hannah's Gate. That makes us all somebodies.'

Keith changed the subject by asking Hank if he was going to get a Christmas tree that morning. Hank said he was, and suggested that Keith go with him.

Elianne only half-listened to them making their plans. She thought of the articles that appeared whenever she went out with Garet. Oh, how she hated to read about Hannah's Gate and the terrible things that had happened there. A chill touched her. Maybe it was true. Maybe the house was cursed, and all the people who lived there were cursed too.

After the holiday, Garet Morley called to ask her to go out to dinner with him. She refused without giving an excuse. In the first week of January, he called again. Once more she refused to see him. He said only that he was sorry she was so busy, but two hours later he appeared at Hannah's Gate.

She first knew of it when Irene led him into the study where ostensibly reading the book in her lap, she had been brooding. It was a new year: 1976. She had returned home five years before. It seemed to her that she was as uncertain, as confused now, as she had been in the day she came back.

Tall and unsmiling, Garet interrupted her thoughts. 'Am I intruding, Elianne?'

She put her book aside, raised her eyes to

his. 'How are you, Garet? I hope you had a good Christmas.'

'I did. And I'm fine. But that isn't the question. I want to know what's wrong. Why are you too busy to see me?'

She felt that she owed him honesty. She said, 'Garet whenever I'm with you something happens. You're an important man. People notice you. I end up in the newspaper, and I hate it.'

'It doesn't matter.'

'But I want to be let alone. I need to be let alone.'

'You're saying you don't want to see me any more,' he said gently. 'Being my friend creates too many problems for you.'

'I . . .' It was just what she meant, but she found that she couldn't say it. It wouldn't be true. She wanted Garet as a friend, but she didn't want to expose herself to any more publicity. She explained as well as she could.

'Then we'll avoid going where we'll be noticed,' he told her.

'No restaurants. No White House dinners,' she said.

He agreed. But she could tell that he wasn't taking her seriously. He would try gradually to talk her into going out with him as before. She knew that she wouldn't change her mind. Once she had been grateful that Garet seemed interested in her. His interest, and her acceptance of it, deflected anyone from thinking of her relationship with Hank. At least that was what she had hoped. Now, faced with the pain of having her life, her family's history, exposed for all the world to exclaim at, she no longer cared.

Garet, however, was willing to accept her terms. He came to Hannah's Gate often. Elianne made sure that they were never alone. Stacy was frequently there. Hank and Keith helped her turn Garet into a family friend. Hers. Hank's. Keith's. David seemed a little in awe of him. Gordon was always polite, but managed to limit their conversations to greetings, discussions of the weather, and an occasional comment about sports.

Elianne felt that she had put behind her all memory of the ugly publicity with Garet, the shooting at the Gaynor house, the disastrous dinner at the White House.

But there lingered within her mind certain phrases. *Tragedy-struck. Multiple murders. The deaths at Hannah's Gate. The curse of Hannah's Gate.* No matter how she tried to obliterate them, they kept coming back to her at odd moments. In waking moments. In her dreams. Now, sensing that the barrier between Hank and her was enlarging, rather than shrinking, she blamed that on Hannah's Gate too. It had begun when they returned home from Death Valley. It had begun *here.*

Still, she needed Hank, loved him. She told herself that with time they would, together, find a way to tear down the invisible wall that separated them.

Then, early in February, she and Hank met in the pool-side cottage. It was the first time in weeks that they were able to be alone to-gether.

After they had made love, she lay in his arms. Oh, it was good to be held like this, to know that Hank needed her as much as she needed him.

Then he said, 'I'm grateful that we have this, Elianne. I always will be. But it isn't enough. I want us to be married, so we won't have to creep down here to be together for a couple of hours.'

She felt as if the blood were slowly draining from her body. A chill current spread down-ward from her cheeks, enveloping her in what felt like icy sheets. She shook violently within the circle of his arms.

Bewildered, he said, 'Elianne, what's the matter?' He took her face by the chin, his dark blue eyes stared into her. 'Why do you look like that?'

'But Hank . . .' she said. 'Hank, I never . . .' She stopped. She didn't know what to say. She loved Hank. She *did* love him, didn't she? Yes, oh, yes. She was certain of her love. But then? Why did she feel this terror, this cold sinking of the heart, when she heard him speak of marriage?

'Elianne, tell me!' Hank was hurt, angry. He sensed her shrinking away from him, even though he still held her.

She stared at him, eyes beseeching. She didn't know. She couldn't explain.

'Why do you look like that?' he kept asking. 'You know I love you. Why is it so extraordinary that I should ask you to marry me?'

'I can't . . . it's not possible . . . Hank, don't spoil everything now.'

'Spoil everything?' He drew away from her, reached for his clothes. 'That's already happened, hasn't it?'

'There's so much . . .'

'Is it your brothers?' he demanded. 'Gordon? David? Are you afraid of them?'

'I don't know. Oh, I'm not afraid of them. I don't mean that. But what would they think and say! What would they do?'

'It shouldn't matter that much, Elianne.'

Maybe it was her brothers. It could be. She knew how difficult Gordon sometimes was. But there was more too, she was beginning to understand. She couldn't marry Hank as long as their separate pasts were barriers between them. Her past at least. Her years away from Hannah's Gate. Taos. The commune called Love City. Jake Babbitt. Those three years when she had been Ella Em. She closed her eyes against a sudden image . . . a shower of splintered glass and a small body tumbling to earth. Hank had never known Ella Em. How could Elianne tell him about her, about those lost three years? And how could she become his wife if she didn't?

'What can your brothers do?' Hank asked. He was dressed now, standing beside the bed on which she sat.

'I don't know,' she said again.

'They can't do anything. You're old enough to be married. They can't stop you.'

They. They. They. Hank didn't understand. Why didn't he? When he said *they* he meant Gordon and David. He didn't know about the rest. And that was what really mattered. Why didn't he know that he didn't know *her,* the real Elianne, Ella Em? Why didn't he realize that she didn't know *him?* Him. The real Hank Ramos?

She said slowly, 'We're lovers, Hank. But we're strangers.'

He shook his head impatiently. 'We aren't strangers, Elianne.' He thought that she was avoiding the question. To him the question was: Would she marry him? If not, why not?

135

He said, 'You do understand, don't you? That they can't stop you?'

'Of course I know that. But I have a responsibility to my brothers, Hank. Gordon is just about twenty, David fifteen even though he looks much older sometimes.' She paused. Then: 'Do you remember how they managed to drive Ollie away? If they knew about us, they would do the same to you.'

'They couldn't.'

The bushes below the window stirred as if a wind had moved through them. But there had been no wind. A shadow slid away from the window and moved silently up the slope to the house.

A door opened, closed. David leaned his shoulder against it. If only Gordon were home. But he was out with Mandy again. He wouldn't be back until much later.

David decided he wouldn't tell Gordon. He didn't deserve to know.

But, at dawn, when Gordon returned, David was in his room, anxiously waiting for him.

After David slipped away from his place beneath the window, Elianne got up. Slowly, her body still trembling, she put on her clothes.

Hank watched her without speaking.

At last she said, whispering, 'I'm sorry, it's spoiled. I can't help it, Hank.'

136

'Nothing's changed.'

'Yes, it is,' she said. 'I'm sorry.' Her eyes brimmed with tears. 'I can't help it, it's over. There's nothing between us any more.'

'Elianne!'

'I can't help it,' she repeated. 'It's how it has to be.' With that she fled from the cottage.

He followed slowly, hurt and bewildered. He knew there was no use arguing now. No amount of discussion would change her mind. Not now. But that didn't mean he was going to give up. He decided to give her time to think about it, and then to bring it up again.

Chapter Seven

Back in mid-January Gordon had brought Carl Utah to meet Elianne, and to ask if she had a job for him. Carl had told her that he was an experienced gardener, and he was good with cars too. In fact, he assured her with a grin, he was an all round handyman. Whatever she needed done at Hannah's Gate, he would do for her. Cleaning up, painting, brick work. Anything. All he wanted was a steady job.

She hadn't thought of having another full-time employee, but she knew there was always plenty to be done. And she was pleased that Gordon had begun to take an interest, so she didn't want to discourage him. Besides, she had liked Carl on sight. She didn't know why. He seemed pleasant, friendly, and there was something familiar about him. She asked where he and Gordon had met, and Carl said they'd run into each other in a place in Georgetown, and started talking. Gordon was a good kid, Carl said, but he needed to settle down a little. Maybe he still had some growing up to do. But after all, he was only twenty years old, wasn't he?

Elianne had agreed to give Carl a trial. He found himself a basement room a few blocks away, and within days it seemed as if he had always been at Hannah's Gate. He set up his own routine, doing what had to be done without orders or suggestions. Soon Elianne was glad that she had followed her instincts and hired him.

Now, in mid-February, he was busy scraping ice off the driveway, and thinking how strange it was for him to be at Hannah's Gate. If he and his wife hadn't broken up, he'd still be living in Oklahoma, doing what he had always done. So he wouldn't have taken the long distance truck driving job that had brought him to Washington in the first place. With his wife gone, and nothing to hold him, no kids, no house, no anything, he figured it didn't matter much where he was. And his curiosity about Hannah's Gate was stronger than ever. He'd read the articles about it, about Elianne. He considered most of what was written a big load of crap. *Tragedy-struck. Strange deaths. A curse on three families.* It made him want to spit. Jesus H. Christ! People died, didn't they? You have three families, there are going to be deaths, aren't there? So what's strange? How was Hannah's Gate different from any other house? Except of course those girls killed by that saboteur. But those murders had nothing to do with the families that belonged to Hannah's Gate. So how could anybody take that baloney seriously?

Still, he knew that Elianne did. She didn't say much, but when Carl had heard Gordon teasing her about her picture in the magazines, he'd seen how it bothered her. Her face grew white, and her eyes bigger than ever. And somehow, during the few weeks since he'd come to work here, he'd seen her change. A brightness had gone out of her face. Shadows darkened her eyes. Carl was pretty sure it had something to do with Hank Ramos. But he didn't know what.

That's why, because she seemed so upset, Carl decided not to tell her about himself. He didn't know what she knew about Casey Loving, but this didn't seem like a good time to spring anything new on her. He'd wait and see.

Now, still thinking about her, he cut some holly boughs from the bushes on the terrace. He wired them together into an arrangement and brought it into the house. From the foyer, he could hear the television set in the study. A newscaster was speaking about the next primary Jimmy Carter was going to run in, with his victory at the Iowa Democratic caucus behind him.

Carl put the holly arrangement on the table, and shrugged. Who cared? What difference would it make?

Inside the study Elianne reached out to switch channels. She too wasn't interested in who was going to be a candidate in the next presidental election.

But Stacy said. 'Hey! Wait! I want to hear this.'

Elianne nodded. They were supposed to be studying for their finals, but another few minutes wouldn't matter.

Stacy was saying. 'It gets fascinating. The politics of it, I mean. Especially since we're in Washington.' When Elianne didn't answer, Stacy went on, 'And specially since I know Garet. I can ask him things. He always knows the answers.'

'I suppose,' Elianne agreed. She reached for her notebook and pushed the dictionary on the end table. It fell to the floor with a heavy thud. From within its pages, a folded sheet of waxed paper slid onto the rug. Elianne picked it up. There were pressed roses within it. One yellow. One white. A wave of sadness swept over her. Roses her mother had kept, probably because Ollie had given them to her.

Elianne asked herself what her mother would say about what had happened between Elianne and Hank. Would she understand? Would she see why Elianne had had to end their affair? Would she have been able to tell her what had gone wrong? Why she felt this way? Empty. Unhappy. As if everything she wanted was gone. Yet she was to blame. She had refused Hank, turned away from him. Because she had to. Had to.

Stacy was silent, listening to the programme. When it was over, she leaned back. 'I guess I'd better tell you, Elianne — I'm going to drop out of school at the end of this term.'

'Stacy! Why? You've only got this next semester, and then you'll graduate.'

'I know, but I'm so bored. And Garet's going to give me a job in his office. I can learn so much that way. Then, when summer comes, I'm going to work in his campaign. He's up for re-election, you know.'

'But you should get your degree,' Elianne protested. 'You're too close to finishing up to drop out now.'

'Oh, degrees,' Stacy said, 'they don't matter any more.'

Elianne realized that Stacy's mind was made up. Nothing she could say would change it now. She decided to let it go.

'Garet's an awfully attractive man,' Stacy told her. 'But I can see why you don't want to go out with him any more. After what happened. Even if it wasn't his fault. Just the same, he's so . . . so good-looking. And everybody respects him. You never know, Elianne. One of these days he might even run for president.'

'He might,' Elianne said. She picked up her notes. 'And we'd better go to work.' As she spoke, she slipped the roses within the waxed paper back into the dictionary, and put it aside.

She and Stacy went over the material together. Meanwhile, with part of her mind, Elianne thought over what Stacy had said. It suddenly began to make sense.

Stacy and Garet had been thrown together at Hannah's Gate a lot. She had become interested in politics, and in him. Her decision to drop out of school to work in his office was a logical further step.

By the end of winter, Elianne rarely heard from Stacy or Garet. When, in late spring she read that the Graysons had announced Stacy's engagement to Garet, she wasn't surprised. That too was a logical further step.

It was a warm April day. A faint haze of green hung over the wistaria beyond the window of Elianne's room. Below, in the pool area, Carl Utah was painting a metal table. A squirrel raced along the brick wall at the foot of the slope.

Elianne tried to picture Hannah's Gate when she was growing up. Mostly she recalled scaffolding and ladders and piles of sand. She couldn't remember when the cabana, now the cottage, had been built, nor when the new wing had been added to the main house. She *did* have a faint recollection of being led through the bomb shelter. But that was all. She supposed there were photographs around that would show what the house had been like in those days. Not that it mattered. What the house had been then had nothing to do with her, with the present. It was part of the past that she didn't want to think about.

She turned away from the window. On her desk there was a pile of bills addressed to Gordon. He had over-spent his allowance by several thousand dollars, and had handed the bills to her for payment from his trust fund. The same thing had been happening regularly for months now. She knew she had to talk to him about it. It was time that he learned how to handle money. If he didn't learn now, he never would. And if he didn't, the trust he would have access to when he turned twenty-five would be dissipated very quickly. If he wasn't ready within the next five years, it would be too late. She didn't care about the money. It was his. Perhaps he had the right to spend it as he wanted to. But what would happen when the trust fund was exhausted? What would he do? He was trained for nothing. He'd graduated from prep school, but still refused to enroll at the university. And what about David? Would he, as he usually did, follow in Gordon's footsteps?

Her thoughts took the same weary path they had travelled before. This time, though, she recalled Foster Talcott saying, 'Gordon's been to see me about increasing his allowance. I referred him to you. Don't do it, Elianne. He's becoming very extravagant and it will only grow worse. Control it now or it will be too late.'

Elianne knew she would have to try, but she didn't know how to deal with Gordon. He would listen, and ignore whatever she told him. And he would continue as before.

Irene interrupted her troubled musing to say that there was someone to see Elianne. He was waiting on the front porch.

Mystified that Irene hadn't brought him in, Elianne said, 'On the porch?'

Irene answered, 'I don't think he belongs in Hannah's Gate.'

Elianne hurried downstairs, and there, on

the porch, in the shadow of the magnolia tree, stood Jake Babbitt.

'Why, Ella Em,' he said, smiling. 'You're certainly looking good. I'm glad to see you again.'

It was five years since she had last seen him. It seemed like much longer to her. In that time, she'd moved from one world to another. That was what she had told herself, what she had believed until this moment. Now she knew that she had deceived herself. The past she had tried so hard to forget was part of the present. It was here, with her, in Hannah's Gate.

Jake looked much older. He was gaunt, his jaw bone showing through the tight skin above his greying beard. He was still tall, but his shoulders were rounded. He wore a thin fringed black denim jacket, torn at both elbows, and dusty black trousers. His tie was a huge bolo on a rawhide string. It was carved from bone in the shape of a human skull.

As his black eyes met hers, time fell away. She stood before him as she had when they first met. Then she had been a frightened fifteen year old, hungry, dirty, tired, and longing for home, but believing that she'd never go back, never could go back.

He waited, then he reached out and gently touched her cheek with one calloused finger,

'What's the matter, Ella Em? Cat got your tongue? Aren't you going to say hello? Aren't you going to invite me in?'

'I'm surprised,' she faltered. 'I just . . . I guess I hardly know where I am.' Her hand went up to touch her hair. It was long and smooth, silky to the touch. She felt it as she had felt it years before. Defiled, hacked away, tufted and bunched and dirty. As her father had left it. As it had been the night she ran away. As it had been the rainy evening when Jake rescued her.

He was saying. 'You're home. That's where you are. And you're fine. Nothing's wrong with you. Not that I can see.' He made an elaborate show of looking around the porch, the grounds, past her into the foyer, where the elegant crystal chandelier tinkled in the warm breeze.

'How did you find me, Jake?'

'I read about you in the paper a while ago, and I wanted to come then.' He shrugged. 'But, as usual, I didn't have the money. So I had to wait.'

'Where were you?'

'In Taos. Where you left me. At Love City.'

She said softly, 'Love City,' she instantly saw the shining veil of broken glass falling from the broken skylight, and tiny Joy's body tumbling through it to the ground. It was that

147

terrible sight that had opened her eyes to the destructiveness of Love City. It was Joy's death that had finally forced her to go home.

'Why?' Elianne asked. 'Why did you come here?'

'You ask a lot of questions these days,' he answered. Then he smiled. 'I see the Divine in every person. Remember that?' At her nod, he went on, 'I see the Divine in you too.'

'I'm a different person now,' she told him. 'I'm Elianne Merrill.'

He scratched his beard thoughtfully. 'I don't think it matters what you call yourself. You're still you.'

She asked, 'What about the group, Jake? What happened?' She was thinking of the two small boys.

He shook his head.

'Do you mean there's nobody left?'

He didn't answer that. Instead he asked, 'Why are you staring at me?'

'I don't know. I think I'm still wondering why you came.'

'Maybe I am too. Maybe I don't know. But the thing is, you look frightened.'

'I suppose I am. A little.'

'Frightened of me? My God, that hurts. How can you be?'

She said nothing.

'Ella Em . . .'

'Don't call me that, Jake!'

'I don't mean you any harm.'

Again she didn't respond.

He leaned down to her, asked persuasively, 'Do you think I do? Tell me. Say the words.'

She couldn't answer him. She knew that he *had* done her harm. But she knew too, now, that she had allowed him to do it. Was he more guilty than she? She didn't know.

'If you think I'm here to hurt you, I'll prove you wrong.'

'Jake,' she said slowly. 'What's this all about?'

'I wanted to see you. So I came.' When she didn't answer, he said, 'Look, don't worry. I'm not going to tell your family anything. Why should I?'

'It's not that.'

'It is. I know.' He smiled briefly. 'I even know that you won't let yourself remember all of it. Because you're scared to.' He touched her shoulder. 'You'd be better off if you stopped pretending you'd never been away. You can try all you want, but you'll never be the girl you were before you met me.'

Once again she saw a shower of glittering glass, and within it, the spinning body of the child. She saw the small form collapse on the red earth. She felt herself choke on tears she couldn't shed. Jake was right. She was no longer the fifteen year old who had lived at Hannah's Gate so long ago. But he was wrong too. She was no longer Ella Em either. She said slowly, 'What do you want of me?'

'Just to see you. It's what I said. Only that.'

She looked beyond him to the van parked in the driveway. Its paint was faded now. A side window was cracked. It had been home to her once. She turned away from it.

He said, smiling, 'Hey, listen, aren't you going to ask me in? I've come a hell of a long way.'

'Of course. Why not?' She tried to sound cordial, welcoming. 'Maybe you'd like something to eat or drink?' She led him inside. She felt so ashamed of herself. She had been wondering how to get rid of him, how to suggest that he leave before anyone else saw him. But he had done everything for her. He had saved her life, fed her, protected her, given her a place to which to belong. Given her a family too, when she needed it. He was part of her, her past. She couldn't send him away. But it was because he was part of her past that she wished so desperately he hadn't appeared.

He stopped under the big chandelier. 'Wow! What a beauty.' He swung around slowly on a run-down boot heel, staring at the wide staircase, the white walls, the gilt-framed mirror over the marble topped table. 'No wonder you came home.'

She took him into the study. He sat in the easy chair, and leaned back to stare at the portrait of Big Jack Gowan. 'Who's the important-looking old geezer?'

'My great-grandfather.'

'I'm impressed.'

'Let me see what I can scare up in the kitchen,' she said.

Jake nodded. He stretched out his legs, making deep impressions in the thick carpet. He was content to sit, and absorb the feeling of the house. The more he looked at Ella Em, at Elianne, the more glad he was that he'd made the trip. From outside the room, he heard voices. He couldn't understand the words. Her family, he supposed. He'd meet them after a while. He was curious, but he wasn't in any hurry. He wasn't going anywhere.

She'd asked him what he wanted. He didn't know. He really didn't know why he'd come. Except that he'd wanted to see her again. It felt good. Seeing her. Being here.

He remembered that he had once said to her: 'My love opens the gates to life.' She hadn't known that Jake invented the phrase, and all the other ones too he offered to her along the way, just as he had invented himself.

For him it began in June of 1964. He was twenty-six years old, an off again on again graduate student. He had volunteered to join a voter registration drive for negroes in Mississippi. He had been trained in Oxford, Ohio, and then, with several hundred others, had been sent to Jackson, Mississippi.

He could remember a special day. Sunny. Warm. The hum of locusts in the damp air. The light achingly bright. He'd been assigned to a group. The three others were Chaney, Schwerner, and Goodman. Chaney, a young negro, was local. Schwerner and Goodman were both Jews from New York. They were going to check out a burned down church, the work, it was thought, of the Ku Klux Klan. Jake dragged himself to where they were waiting for him beside a Ford station wagon. He told them he couldn't go. Not that day. He was having a bad belly ache, the kind that wouldn't allow him to take a long car trip. They understood. They grinned, commiserated, and drove away into Neshoba County. And vanished from the face of the earth.

When Jake heard that they had disappeared, he knew they were dead. By then, his belly ache was gone. He had a new ache in him. He knew they'd been killed. He saw their faces before him. The dark one. The two white ones. All grinning. He kept thinking that he should have been with them. Whatever had happened to them, should have happened to him.

In August the three bodies were found. They had been shot. Their joint memorial stone had been only six miles from Philadelphia, Mississippi, the freshly built earthen dam in which their bodies had been hidden.

Before the death of the three, Jake had known who he was. With their going, he was lost. His past, the man he had been then, was dead too. He no longer knew hope nor faith. He dropped out of the registration drive. He dropped out of school. He went on the road.

By December, when twenty-one Neshoba County men were arrested for involvement in the murder of the three, Jake had already begun to invent himself, and to make up a new language in which he could express what he felt, and to look for a new life in which he could forget the cruelty of the one he had turned from.

He found a piece of land outside of Taos, in the hills of north-eastern New Mexico. He settled in a leanto he built himself. Slowly he gathered to him a small group. He taught it in his new language. The place was called Love City. The language was the word of love.

For him, it was an act of salvation. He had

been betrayed by his bowels. Because of a belly ache he hadn't gone with Chaney and Schwerner and Goodman to look at the burned down church. So he was the only one to have survived. His survival required explanation and expiation. He conceived his creed to satisfy himself. In the years since he had stayed and the three others had gone, he had invented Jake Babbitt . . .

Now he smiled to himself, reached absently for his pouch and cigarette papers. He started to roll one. Then he realized what he was doing. Oh, no. Not here. Not now. Certainly not until he saw how the wind was blowing.

As he returned pouch and paper to his pocket, Elianne came back with a tray.

'Chicken salad,' she said. 'Okay? And tea?' She set the tray on the table beside him.

'Good,' he told her, after the first bite. He slanted a look at her face. 'Remember how we used to eat rice? And noodles? And then more rice?'

'It was a long time ago,' she said sombrely.

'Sure. But that doesn't mean I can't remember.'

When he had finished, he thanked her. She was startled. She couldn't remember that Jake had ever said 'thank you' for anything. Her memory of his matter of fact acceptance of anything, everything, was built on a thousand small images. Jake Babbitt was the leader, the father, the preacher. He said thank you only to the Divine, and the Divine was love, his love, his disciples' love. Had she ever believed in him, believed in that love? She wasn't sure. She thought that she might never have believed in anything, that only simple fear had kept her with him, and that that same simple fear had grown to unmanageable proportions that had finally driven her away from him.

He sat looking at her, and finally said, 'I need to tell you again. I'm not here to hurt you, and I won't.'

'I know that, Jake,' she answered. But her voice sounded different to her. It was thin, shaking, childish. It was her Ella Em voice. She cleared her throat hard, and said it again. 'I know that.'

'Then don't look so worried.'

She didn't answer him. At the sound of voices below the window, she went to look.

Gordon and David were standing on the terrace. Mandy Sommers was with them. They were watching Carl Utah work at the pool.

Mandy had been to the house many times in the past few months. She had come to feel very much at home there. She raised an acknowledging hand to Elianne, who nodded, and turned back to Jake.

Within moments, Gordon and Mandy came in.

Elianne introduced them to Jake. He rose, towering over Gordon. Next to Gordon, Jake looked disreputable and dangerous. Next to Jake, Gordon looked like a plump but polished adolescent. Jake shook Gordon's hand, smiled into Mandy's eyes.

Gordon immediately launched into a series of questions disguised as friendly and enthusiastic curiosity. They began with, 'Where are you from?' and ended with, 'And what are you doing here?'

Jake was in no way fooled. He answered, half-answered, and ignored whatever he didn't care to deal with. When he tired of the interrogation, he rose again, yawned and stretched. 'What I need is a good nap. I've come a long way.'

Elianne said nothing.

He grinned at her. 'A place this size . . . surely you've got a spare bed I can use for a few hours?'

Gordon made a faint protesting sound. But Mandy linked her arm through his, drew him away, saying, 'Gordie, I want to go down to the cottage.'

They left Jake and Elianne, and went along the terrace, and down the slope to the pool area. As they passed Carl Utah, she gave him a long sideways look. A faint smile. Her hips moved in an exaggerated swing. It was a habit with her. As long as there were men around, Mandy was aware of them.

Clinging to Gordon's arm, she remembered her first visit to Hannah's Gate. She'd swung her legs out of the car, looking admiringly at the magnolia near the front porch, and the wide spread of soft green grass. A squirrel had raced along the top of the wall, stopped to look at her, then hurried away.

Gordon had taken her through the house. He had shown her the portrait of Big Jack Gowan in the study, the dining room and the kitchen, where Irene greeted him brusquely. She had stared at Mandy, and then turned back to her stove. Gordon had taken Mandy down to the cottage and told her about when he and David were small, the games they had played there. He didn't mention Ollie, or his mother, or the time they had lived in the cottage together. He had said the cottage was rarely used these days. Perhaps it should be converted back to a playroom again.

She had been enthusiastic about that then, imagining herself lying beside the pool, her red bikini brilliant against her tanned skin.

Now, though, she suddenly had another idea. She led Gordon through the cottage again. 'It's so nice as it is,' she said. 'A real little nest. Just perfect for two.' She saw herself living there with Gordon. Their own place. At Hannah's Gate.

'Who's the girl?' Jake was asking.

'She's a friend of Gordon's.'

'I thought so,' Jake said. He yawned. 'So what about it, Ella Em? How about I have a little nap? A few hours rest?'

'Don't call me that!' she cried.

'Okay. Sorry, Elianne.' But he was smiling at her.

She smiled back. 'I'm being silly.'

'I guess you are.'

She couldn't think of any way to tell him that he couldn't stay, that she didn't want him in Hannah's Gate. He got his backpack from the van, and then she led him to a room in the new wing.

He set the backpack on the dresser, took a long look around. 'Nice.'

'Jake,' she said. 'There's one thing . . . I don't want anything here. In this house.'

'Anything?'

'You know what I mean. No . . . no dope. None. Nothing. I'm finished with it. I don't want it around.'

'Sure,' he said. 'Don't worry. I understand.' He smiled at her. 'Actually I'm clean. Absolutely.'

158

★ ★ ★

He had said he needed a few hours' rest. He was still there the next morning.

Within a few days, Elianne realized that he didn't intend to move on. He planned to stay. For how long, she couldn't guess.

When, finally, she asked him, he said, 'I don't know, Elianne. I'm thinking. Just give me some time.' His smile was bright within his beard. 'You've got plenty of time, haven't you? Along with plenty of space.'

He didn't say, 'And money, too,' but she knew that was what was in his mind.

'But what are you going to do, Jake?'

'Do?'

'About your life?'

'I need to start again. I've been lost. I must find the way again.' He was silent for a moment before he went on, 'I think we must learn from our mistakes. We must build with love. That will be the Divine.'

She said gently, regretfully, 'You've told me that before.'

He blinked at her. He hadn't expected her to say that. It was out of character for Ella Em. But Ella Em had changed. And she was right. He'd said the same thing before. He had no new idea. He was here because he wanted to see her. He had no plan. He had nothing to think about. He wasn't ready to

159

go on, so he wouldn't. It was all very simple to him.

She stared at him, remembering what he had said, 'You go to him, because I tell you to go to him. We share all we have. We share our love, and our bodies. You go to him.' And he had turned to other girls, new ones, bold and laughing ones. She armoured herself in those memories, certain that nothing about him had changed.

She told herself that she should explain that he must make plans about leaving. The best thing to do would be to set a date. She found it impossible to do. Whenever she nerved herself to it, she would remember what he had done for her. The good that he had done. And her heart shrivelled inside her. He knew his Ella Em, even if she was changed. And he made sure, with a hundred tiny hints, that he too recalled for her everything he had done. The good. And the bad. And all that she had done as well.

Meanwhile, he used the days to explore the city. He learned the geography of Washington and Georgetown. He wandered through the streets, pausing to talk to the street musicians and flower vendors. He looked in all the shop windows. Most of his time was spent that way. However he always came back to Hannah's Gate, either for a meal or a night's sleep.

* * *

Within the first week of Jake's arrival, Gordon realized that their guest had no intention of leaving soon. He told David, 'We'd better be careful. Jake Babbitt is a trouble maker.'

But he had already figured out, with prompting from Mandy, how to use Jake's presence to his own advantage.

Chapter Eight

Mandy lay beside the pool on a warm Sunday afternoon. It was just as she had pictured it. She wore a red bikini, a new one from Saks Wisconsin Avenue that Gordon had bought for her after she wistfully told him about it. She had also wistfully told him about a string of pearls at Pamplonia's, and an assortment of shoes and bags at Gucci in the Watergate. The pearls were in her dresser, in the cottage. So were the shoes and bags.

She had moved in ten days before, and felt as if she'd lived at Hannah's Gate forever.

Now, soaking up the early May sun, she watched through half-closed eyes as Hank wheeled Keith to the pool area. She scarcely noticed Keith, his useless legs covered by a thin white sheet. It was Hank she stared at. He was a very good-looking hunk of man. Too bad he didn't have anything but his lousy job playing nursemaid to the cripple. Why did he do it? What made him waste his time and his looks? Men like him, girls like her, they deserved everything. And had nothing.

But Mandy was determined to change that. All she needed was a little time. Pretty soon, she told herself, she'd have everything. Gordie would see to that.

It had been easy to get him to persuade her that they should live together. He didn't even realize that it had been her idea and not his. As soon as she saw that Jake Babbitt was there, and settling in for good, or at least for a long, long stay, she'd seen how to handle it. It worked out just the way she thought it would.

Gordon didn't ask Elianne. He moved his own things to the cottage. Then he moved Mandy's clothes in. One day she was a guest, coming for a few hours' visit, for a swim in the pool, and a lunch prepared by Irene. The next day Mandy was a permanent resident.

Soon after, she quit her job. All she had to do was concentrate on keeping Gordon happy and interested in her. She managed to evade having breakfast with the family by insisting that she never ate early in the morning. She and Gordon went to the big house for dinner a couple of times a week because she had convinced Gordon they had to.

Elianne told him he was too young to have a live-in girl friend. He smiled at her. She said he had no right to bring someone to live at Hannah's Gate without discussing it first with her. He continued to smile while he reminded her that she hadn't discussed Jake with anybody. Yet Jake was there. Mandy had told him that he'd get more flies with honey than with vinegar, and he was determined to remember that. When Elianne blushed at his mention of Jake, Gordon just smiled more widely. She said, 'I'm not sleeping with Jake.'

Gordon said nothing. He didn't mention Hank. He didn't need to. After that one time, Elianne didn't protest any more about Mandy.

He laughed when he told Mandy about it. He laughed somewhat less when he saw that Mandy was flirting with Hank, with Jake, even with old, ankle-sprung Carl Utah. Flirting, flaunting herself. On occasion, she even tried it out on David, saying, 'I love robbing the cradle,' shooting a sly look at Gordon, 'so one of these days, it's going to be your turn, David.'

David would flush a deep red. His eyes would narrow beneath lowered lids, as if tears had filled them. He would swallow so hard that his Adam's apple would bob up and down in his thin throat.

He would hurry away, Mandy's laughter following him. In his mind, silently, he'd curse her. Bitch! Damned bitch! Why did Gordon have to have her around? What did Gordon see in her? Until she'd come along, David and Gordon had been close, two halves of the same coin. Now they were split down the middle. There had been the two of them against Elianne. Now David was nothing. Gordon and Mandy were one.

But David kept watching Mandy. He couldn't help himself.

Gordon watched her too. He fumed, and sulked. When fuming and sulking didn't work, he bribed her by buying her more gifts. He was so infatuated with her that he couldn't blame her for his jealousy, so he blamed Elianne. It was Elianne's fault that Mandy winked at Keith, dragged Hank into a few quick dance steps, ran her slim fingers through Jake's beard, and patted David's cheek. It was Elianne's fault that Mandy even swung her hips at Carl Utah while he worked around the grounds. Gordon was angry at the men, but he told himself it would be okay, except for Elianne. Because, after all, it was her fault that he was not master of Hannah's Gate. And if he were, everything would be different.

David, listening to Gordon's complaints, agreed. Of course, it was all Elianne's fault.

Keith was in his bedroom. When he had come to Hannah's Gate to live after his father's death, Claire had decorated for Keith the room

165

that had once been Rea's. She had taken advantage of its long narrow shape to give it the look of two rooms. At one end there was a deep wide loveseat, a table, and a big easy chair in front of the television set. At the other end she had put the bed, the dresser, and end table. There was plenty of room between the furniture, so that Keith could manipulate his wheel chair. There were lots of bookshelves, where he stored his books and games and records.

Keith looked across the room at Hank, watching him shift in the easy chair. Cross his legs. Stretch. Re-cross them in the other direction. He wriggled his shoulders and reached behind him to adjust the lamp so that the light fell more directly on the page of the book he held.

Keith understood his restlessness. He must be thinking about Elianne. Keith didn't know that she had ended the affair. He sensed his friend's moodiness and supposed it was because Hank and Elianne had no opportunity to get together any more. Everything had changed, Keith thought, since Mandy had come to Hannah's Gate. And Jake's arrival had only made it worse. Keith had suggested that Hank take Elianne out, to dinner or a movie, insisting that he could easily manage alone for an evening. But Hank had refused to do that. So the two were stuck in the house. The cottage was no longer available. And there were too many people around for them to find even an hour's privacy.

Now Hank closed his book. He fixed his eyes on the opposite wall, drumming his fingers on the chair arm.

Keith said, 'Listen, Hank, you can take a walk if you want to.' he added quickly, 'Stay on the grounds, if that'll make you feel better.'

Hank shook his head, but then, as he looked out of the window, he saw Elianne move across the terrace below. Maybe now he could talk to her. She'd avoided him so insistently. But now, when she was alone . . . Hank got up quickly. 'You'll be all right?'

'Sure. I'll sit here and read. Take your time. I'm not sleepy. I don't want to go to bed yet.' He was comfortable in the wheel chair. A jug of water, and a glass on the table close by. He didn't need anything.

'Okay,' Hank said. 'I'll be back in an hour or so.'

After he had gone, Keith read a word or two. Then he closed his book. He wheeled himself to the window, pushed back the curtain. He could see the terraces, the long slope down to the pool, and the lights in the cottage.

As he watched, he saw Hank catch up with Elianne. He put a hand on her arm. She

167

stopped, shook her head, and went on walking, more quickly this time. Hank kept pace with her. In the dim light from one of the downstairs windows, Keith saw the blur of her face. But he couldn't see her expression. He hoped she was smiling, happy. More than anything, he wanted that. She was so good to him, the sister he'd never had. He wanted Hank to be happy too. Keith was sure they were right for each other. Lately Hank had been too quiet, depressed even. Elianne was different too. Maybe it had to do with Mandy or Jake. Keith couldn't figure it out. But that was why he was so anxious for Hank to have time alone with Elianne. He knew they loved each other. He thought that Hank could mend whatever it was, if he had the chance. And tonight he did. He and Elianne disappeared into the darkness at the corner of the new wing.

As Keith started to swing away from the window, he saw a tall slim figure separate itself from the shadows. it moved slowly, silently, following along the path that Elianne and Hank had taken.

Keith let his breath out in a long sigh. Damn! Damn! That was no good. It was David. Spying again. He'd done it before, Keith knew. Keith had seen him crouched below the cottage window when Elianne and

Hank were there. That was before Mandy moved in. What had David wanted then? What did he want now? Why was he following Hank and Elianne? Why couldn't he leave them alone?

Below, in the shadows beyond the new wing, Elianne stopped. She drew back from Hank's touch. 'No,' she said in a tense whisper. 'No, Hank. I don't want to talk.'

After long sleepless nights, thinking of Hank, wanting him, she had settled it in her mind. She had ended their affair. She would no longer dream of him. Since Jake's coming, her confusion had grown. Memories of him intruded. His body, hairy and bony, and his words, flowing, chanting, singing. She didn't want to compare the two men. They had nothing to do with each other. She didn't want to remember being with Jake. He belonged to the dead past, to Ella Em. If Ella Em had loved him then, that love had died when she died. Elianne loved Hank now. But with that thought a painful doubt bloomed within her. Love. What did she know of it? Had she loved those others that she'd been with? The ones Jake had told her to go to? The few she had chosen for herself? Could she pretend that she had loved all of them?

Now she thought she had found love with Hank. How did she know? With Jake, and with the others, she had taken the need to be cared for and protected as love. She had felt the need to be alive, and considered that love.

How could she love Hank and be so terrified when he said he wanted to marry her? What did that mean?

Hank said desperately, 'Elianne, you have to listen to me.'

'I can't,' she said despairingly. 'I made a mistake. I'm sorry. I thought I . . . I thought I was in love with you, but . . . now . . . now I see I was wrong. We can't go back to the way it was in Death Valley. I'm sorry. Pretend it never happened, Hank.'

Turning away she ran up the path and into the house.

Chapter Nine

That night, as he settled Keith in bed, Hank told himself that he wasn't finished. He wasn't going to give up until he understood what had changed Elianne.

But it was impossible to talk to her at breakfast. David was there when Hank brought Keith in. Jake too.

Elianne looked at Hank over one of Carl's flower centrepieces, and finished her coffee. She got up saying, 'I'll be late coming home. I have to go to the library.'

Hank couldn't speak to her that evening either. After dinner, when the family had gathered, she went immediately to her room, saying that she had to study.

Hank waited an hour, then tapped at her door. He told her that Irene was going to spend the evening with Keith. He was free, and wanted her to go out with him so that they could talk.

She said, 'There's nothing to talk about,

Hank.' and closed the door in his face.

He waited a few moments, then tapped again. From within, he heard her say, 'Hank, go away!'

Since Keith would be taken care of for the evening, Hank decided to go out. He went to Charlie Carroll's house. Charlie and his wife Amy gave him coffee and pie. But Hank was restless. Charlie saw that and suggested that the two of them go out for a couple of beers.

Charlie had the beer, but Hank had whisky. It didn't help, but he drank it anyway. They talked about Charlie's detective business, about the city. Finally Charlie asked, 'Anything special on your mind?'

Hank shook his head. He wasn't going to say anything about Elianne. In fact, what was there to say? They'd had an affair. Now she'd called it quits. It was something that happened all the time. That's how it was. That's what had happened. He wished he understood *why* it had happened. But if she wouldn't explain, she wouldn't.

He supposed he should leave Hannah's Gate, but he didn't intend to. Keith needed him. It wouldn't be easy to find someone reliable to look after Keith; there was not only the physical part but the mental part too. Hank knew how important it was for Keith to keep on studying. So leaving Hannah's Gate was out. He kept asking himself what had changed Elianne. Was it because he'd asked her to marry him? Or was it Jake? Was it her brothers? Why wouldn't she explain? He hated so many unanswered questions. He made himself stop thinking about them.

Near the booth where Charlie and Hank sat, there were five men at a round table. Hank could hear their conversation. It was about Vietnam.

Hank and Charlie exchanged glances, and Charlie said softly. 'Still going over it . . . nobody ever forgets. Nobody. Ever.'

Hank shook his head, stared into his glass. Suddenly a deep aching guilt was the clutch of icy fingers at his heart, a tightening until he had no breath left in him.

'And it's the same with you,' Charlie said. 'Bien Kok.'

'Yes.' Hank raised his eyes to Charlie's face. 'I try not to, but I keep thinking about it. I keep trying to remember.'

'So it never came back?'

'Most of it did. But not the important thing. Not what I did. I see everything else as if it was yesterday. But me, what I did, that's the blank.'

Charlie whistled softly. 'You mean that's what you don't remember? Hank, I can't believe this. I didn't realize until you told me just now . . . Listen, don't you understand? You didn't *do* anything. That's the point. I know. I was right there with you. You didn't do anything at all.'

'I had the gun. I remember that,' Hank said miserably.

Charlie nodded, leaned forward. His face was earnest. His eyes looked directly into Hank's. He said in a slow flat voice, 'Sure you remember that. You were holding the damn thing, and firing at the sky. At the sky, man! You never hit anything. Not even a tree!'

For a single long instant Hank was chilled with disbelief. How could it be? 'Are you sure?' he asked hoarsely. 'You're not just saying . . . ?'

'I'm sure,' Charlie said. 'God, man! How could I lie about that to you?'

Now the disbelief was gone. Charlie's certainty was suddenly Hank's. Charlie had been there. He'd seen. He knew. And, as he said, how could he lie to Hank?

The certainty was blessed relief. The weight he'd carried for so long was suddenly gone. He was free. He emptied his glass. He leaned back in his chair, laughing softly. 'What do you know? I didn't do anything! It doesn't matter what I remember, or what I've forgotten. I didn't do anything! I didn't even hit a tree!'

He felt wonderful. He had never been stronger. He told himself that everything was going to be all right. He'd fix whatever had happened. He'd make Elianne change her mind. Somehow he'd win her back again.

A few days later Elianne hurried home from school. Finals would begin in a week. She had a lot of studying to do, and a paper to write. Her mind went back to the previous term. She and Stacy had gone over the material together, quizzing each other on dates. That was when Stacy had told her about the job with Garet, and her plan to drop out of school. Now Stacy and Garet were engaged.

The mail was on the table in the foyer next to one of Carl's fresh flower arrangements. Yellow and white roses, her mother's favourites, Elianne thought. She took the envelopes with her to the kitchen. As she had a glass of milk, she went through them. Mostly there were advertisements. But one thick envelope was from Foster Talcott. He had forwarded to her a stack of Gordon's bills. Bills that Gordon had been unable to pay from his monthly allowance. Foster included a note suggesting that Elianne have a talk with Gordon. He didn't tell her what to say to her brother. He also didn't tell her what she should do about the cheques Gordon had written on a non-existent bank account.

She finished her milk and suddenly raised her head. The house was quiet, so quiet that the sound of her own breathing was audible. She realized that this wasn't the first time she had listened to the silence. There had been many moments in these last few months when she had noticed a strange quality in the house. It was as if, briefly, life stood still. And always, in that space of empty time, she sensed a waiting. Was it in her mind? She didn't know. Could she be imagining it? Yes, of course. Still she couldn't shake the feeling of uneasiness it engendered in her. Then, even as she became aware of it, the moment would pass. It happened that way this time too. There was the waiting silence, the emptiness. She heard the sound of Keith's voice. He was saying something about Woodward and Bernstein, a book called *The Final Days*.

Thinking about how much she had to do, she took her mail and went upstairs. Soon at her desk, she reached for the research notes she had prepared for her paper. The box in which she had left them was empty. She frowned, puzzled. She *had* left them in the box, hadn't she? She rose, pushed the desk from the wall, thinking that perhaps they'd fallen behind it. No. Nothing. She opened the top drawer, went through everything. No again. She checked the whole desk, systematically taking everything out, examining it, then putting it back. The notes weren't there. She hurried to the cupboard. Perhaps she had absent-mindedly left them on a shelf. Ever since she had broken off with Hank she had found her mind wandering. Her thoughts returned continually to him. She told herself to concentrate. She had to find the notes. The shelves held only a few bags, pairs of shoes, the wide-brimmed hat she sometimes used at the pool. She got down and looked under the bed. She even opened the medicine cabinet in her bathroom, and went through the clothes hamper too. The notes were gone.

She supposed that somehow she had thrown them away. But how could she have? It had taken her so long to dig up the material. Without it she couldn't write her paper. If she didn't turn the paper in, she wouldn't pass the course. She might not graduate. She couldn't believe it had happened. Once again, she examined her desk, her room. It was no use. The material had disappeared.

She went down to the kitchen to ask if Irene had seen it, maybe Elianne had left it somewhere in the house and Irene had found it and forgotten to mention it. But Irene knew nothing about the notes.

Elianne did the only thing she could do. She

dragged out all the books she had used, and stayed up all night, getting the material together for the second time. She worked feverishly on her report, and finished it in time.

Three days later, she accidentally came upon a few shreds of white, blue-lined paper, with rain-streaked writing on them, in a puddle beneath a rose bush behind the house.

Examining them, she recognized her handwriting in the few legible words. At least she knew her notes were truly gone, not just mislaid. They had been destroyed. Someone had taken them deliberately. But why? To hurt her? Who had done it? Gordon or David? Mandy? Jake? Carl Utah? Any one of them could have slipped into her room. It was never locked. But why would any of them want to hurt her? To delay her graduation from school? She pressed her hands to her temples. Her head ached. She didn't dare think about it for too long. She tried to forget about it.

She wanted to forget about Gordon's unpaid bills too. But she knew that she would have to talk to him.

One evening, as the family finished dinner, she asked him to join her in the study. He agreed, and as Mandy made as if to follow him, Elianne said, 'Just the two of us, Gordon.'

'Sure,' he said easily. And to Mandy: 'I'll be along in a minute.' When they were alone in the study he asked Elianne what it was all about. Her sour face. Her wanting to see him by himself.

She told him about the bills Foster Talcott had sent to her, about the cheques written on a non-existent bank account. She said, 'Gordon, you must live within your means. Your allowance is substantial. You should be able to manage comfortably on it.'

He reddened, his eyes narrowing to shining slits. But he said sheepishly, 'I know, Elianne. I guess I've been going overboard, haven't I?' He was thinking of Mandy. Mandy who said, *Honey, Gordon. Honey. It gets more flies than vinegar any day.*

Relief at his reaction made Elianne laugh. 'I guess you have.'

'I'll be more careful,' he promised. 'Just give me a break this time. It won't happen again.'

But later, when he told David about it, he didn't smile.

Elianne graduated from college at the end of May, but she didn't attend the ceremonies, although Keith and Hank had tried to talk her into it.

To celebrate the event, Keith suggested that they go to Skyline Drive in Virginia, for a weekend. 'The three of us. Like in Death Valley. Remember how good that was?'

179

He thought it would be a chance for Hank and Elianne to be alone away from Hannah's Gate. He hoped that whatever had gone wrong between them would be mended, given the opportunity.

Hank and Elianne exchanged glances at Keith's words, then both looked away quickly. But she said finally that she'd like a weekend away.

They started out on a bright early June day in Keith's van. Hank drove, with Elianne beside him. Keith sat in the back in his special seat.

Elianne felt good that she had finished school. One goal was behind her. She had never thought, when she came home five years before, that she would be able to do it. If only her mother were here to enjoy this with her, and to know that her encouragement had paid off.

She slid a glance at Hank. He was very quiet. She wondered what he was thinking. Their affair now seemed distant as a dream. Still, she had the desire to touch him, his hand, his cheek. But it would be useless, and would only give him the wrong idea. It was over between them. What there had been was over. Ella Em's love . . . if only he hadn't asked her to marry him, then maybe they could have gone on as before. But now, now it had to be finished.

The shining fields rolled by, soon became forested with apple orchards, the leaves still the pale green of early growth. The fruit was too small to be observed from the road. Along the way they saw meadows of wild flowers: blue gentian and Queen Anne's lace and Indian paintbrush. They passed through Warrenton and then tiny Washington, Virginia, and soon began climbing, the road, rising in long narrow curves beneath hills of grey stone, where mountain laurel and maple trees had made precarious holds for themselves.

It took them three hours to reach Big Meadows, a low fieldstone building a mile off the drive, with a fine view of the Shenandoah Valley and the massed blue-shrouded hills of the Massanutten range.

They had reserved a two-room log cabin. Hank and Keith shared one, and Elianne had a room to herself. The accommodation was simple but comfortable.

The dining room was in the main lodge. It was high-ceilinged, with glass walls on one side, and exposed wooden beams. A large stone fireplace dominated the other side. In the basement there was a small bar, a few tables, and a tiny stage where entertainers sometimes played the guitar and sang mountain folk songs.

After dinner Keith and Hank and Elianne spent a few hours there. Then Keith said he wanted to go back to the cabin. They returned with him. Soon Elianne left the two men.

Hank let half an hour pass. He had been waiting for just such an opportunity as this. Ever since his talk with Charlie Carroll he'd been thinking about Elianne, about himself. She'd once said to him that they were strangers to each other. He realized now how true that was. The central point of his life had been the nightmare of Bien Kok. He hadn't been able to talk about that. So he hadn't been able to talk about anything related to his past. He was, more than she had imagined, a stranger to her. She must feel the need to talk about what had happened in her years away from home, but she never had. He was sure there had to be a reason for that. Whatever had happened in those years didn't matter to him, but she would always feel a stranger to him unless she was able to talk to him about them. Or, and he thought that most important, unless she was able to forget them completely. He knew that was unlikely as long as Jake Babbitt, a relic of that past, Hank was certain, remained at Hannah's Gate.

Still, Hank was determined. He was going to change her mind. He told Keith he'd be back in an hour, and then went to knock at

Elianne's door. When she opened it, he said, 'Come out for a few minutes, Elianne. We have to talk.' At her hesitation, he went on, 'I'm not your enemy. You've nothing to fear from me. And I don't have the plague. I want you to remember that I'm me. Hank. Even if I'm not your lover any more, I remain your friend.'

She followed him out of the cabin, and they walked side by side, into the shadows.

When Keith heard the outer door close, he rolled himself to the window. He watched as Hank and Elianne went down the walk, past the parking lot, and into the trees. They moved slowly, not touching, Elianne's face turned to Hank's. It made Keith feel good to see them.

Now, when they were alone, they'd have a chance to talk it out. They'd fix it. So Hank's smile could be natural instead of forced. So Elianne could laugh again as if she really was happy, and not pretending.

Then, as Keith watched, he saw a tall slim form emerge from behind a pickup truck. Although it was shrouded in darkness, although it was faceless, he recognized the shape of the head. It was David.

What was he doing here? Why had he come? Why was he spying on Hank and Elianne again? Keith's hands clenched. If only he could move! Do something! Stop him!

But Keith was trapped in the chair. It was no use. He could do nothing now. He leaned back, closed his eyes. He had to think. Surely there was a way to make David leave them alone?

They walked beneath silent pines, making soft scuffing noises with every step. Small animals were startled into sudden flight. An occasional white moth rose up to flutter past their faces.

Hank tried to think of the right way to begin, but the words wouldn't come to him. At last he plunged in, saying, 'Elianne all this time we've known each other — we haven't really, have we?'

She gave him a wary look.

'You said it yourself: that we were strangers.' When she still didn't speak, he hurried on, 'You see, there was something I couldn't talk about.' He drew a deep breath. Then, very slowly, he told her about his life in Vietnam. About Bien Kok. He described for her the boy he had been before, growing up at Big Sur, in the flower-surrounded inn that had skidded away off the mountain and into the ocean. He described for her the man he had become after Bien Kok. The man who came to Washington to work for Charlie Carroll, who had decided to care for Keith because he had to do something. He explained how in caring for Keith he'd found that he was healing himself. When, finally, he had run out of words, he stopped and took her by the arm. He looked down into her face. 'Do you understand now?'

She nodded. 'I understand, Hank. And thank you. But . . . oh, Hank, try to forgive me — I can't help it. I just made a mistake. I . . . can't be in love. I don't want to be.'

'I'll help you. I promise, Elianne.'

'No,' she cried. 'No. You can't!'

'Is it Jake?' he asked.

'Jake?' she repeated, her voice breaking. 'Oh, no!' Then, sharply, she cried, 'Let's go back, Hank. It's no use.'

Pink dawn light filled the sky when Elianne awakened. She was tired. She wished she could go back to sleep but she couldn't, and lying in bed only gave her time to remember the night before. Hank's voice, deep and slow, telling her about Bien Kok. His fear at what he had done. Oh, how it had hurt to know that she was hurting him. She had to move, to get away from her thoughts. She rose, showered and dressed, and hurried outside. Although she wore a jacket, the air was cold now. But it was sweet with the scent of fresh-cut grass and newly-budding trees. The western sky was just beginning to lighten, a sprinkle of stars still shining. Above the tree tops to the east, the pink was fading to morning gold.

She went down the path beyond the cluster of log cabins. Within moments she had passed the ledge, and its parking lot, and picked up a spur that would lead to the Appalachian trail. Very quickly she was deep in the forest. There was a rustling of birds, awakening and stirring in the trees above her. Sounds came from the brush. Yet a special quietness engulfed her as she followed the trail down the hillside, zigzagging along narrow switchbacks in her descent.

There were louder sounds from the growth. She thought of bears. Was one stalking her? Or could there be a mountain lion following her scent? She laughed at herself. True, there were bears in the Blue Ridge Mountains. But if she didn't bother them, they wouldn't bother her. As for mountain lions . . . she supposed it was possible, but not very likely.

Yet she had the feeling that she was being watched. At last the sensation became so strong that she decided to turn back.

She hurried, suddenly hot with apprehension, suddenly breathless. At the top of a switchback, with the mountainside looming over her, and a single huge rock tilted over a stony ridge above her, she stopped to rest.

The sky was still blue and gold. The angle of the huge grey rock seemed to alter, turning against the sky as she looked at it. Suddenly the trees above her quivered and thrashed wildly. Without thought or plan, she lunged to one side, stumbling over a fallen log, and tumbling, out of control, down and down, into a deep bed of pine needles.

Even as she fell, the skyline above was forever changed. The grey rock came roaring, crashing, bounding down the hill, crushing the brush, smashing trees, thundering by in a dusty wind, with fading echoes trailing it as it plunged into the ravine below.

The place where she had stood on the path was crushed and broken, the dust settling slowly on formless leaves and splintered trees and flattened brush.

Eyes widening, she stared at it. If she hadn't thrown herself aside . . . she could hear the deep wracking sobs of her breath. Otherwise there was no sound except the soft rustling of the settling forest. She pushed herself to her feet. Dirt-streaked, sweating, she hurried up the path and out of the trees, on to the spur that led to the road. By then the sun had fully risen. Yellow rays streaked the sky. A group of hikers came towards her, eyeing her curiously as they went by.

Before she got to the cabin, she smoothed her hair and plucked from it some debris. She dried the sweat from her face. But she was still plainly dishevelled and shaken, in spite of her efforts, as she went into the cabin.

Hank and Keith were there, waiting for her. Hank cried, 'Elianne! What happened!'

She laughed shakily, trying not to make too much of her experience. 'It was crazy. I was walking along the trail, and heard a noise. And I looked up, still walking, and fell over a log. It's a good thing I did too because a big rock broke loose and came straight down at me, at where I'd been standing before I fell.'

'Are you sure you're all right?' Hank asked.

'Oh, yes. It just scared me a little.'

Keith listened and watched with a sinking heart. He remembered the night before. The shadow drifting slowly through the dark, following Elianne and Hank . . . Had that same shadow followed Elianne this morning?

Later, when Elianne and Keith were playing cards, Hank went down the trail that she had taken. It was easy for him to find the place where the boulder had come down. He climbed up to the spot from which it had fallen. He stood there, studying the ridge, while orange butterflies sailed and looped from bush to bush, and honey bees darted by.

He wished Charlie Carroll were with him. Maybe the detective's trained eyes would see something he himself might miss. But what he did see was a shallow pit where the boulder had once stood. The earth in it was still damp, black and fresh. Nearby, right at its edge but at right angles to it, there was a short length of heavy tree trunk. Next to that lay a thick iron lathe: old, rusted, long-abandoned. Hank picked it up, laid it over the tree trunk, and moved it in a see-saw motion. It would have been easy, using the iron lathe and the tree trunk for leverage, to free the boulder and send it tumbling down towards Elianne.

It would have been easy, but had it been done? Hank asked himself. Was that what had happened? He knelt to go over the ground carefully. It was hard to tell. There were several footprints. Were they old or new?

He remembered being point man on patrol, kneeling just as he did now, staring with burning eyes at the roiled earth. And at the same time, listening, the pulse beating in his throat, his head. The familiar fear . . . But now it was for Elianne. Could he be imagining this? Why had he come here in the first place? What made him think that Elianne was in danger?

Sighing, he turned to go back to Big Meadows Lodge. He didn't know why he was so uneasy. He didn't know why he had come out to the trail to look at the place where Elianne had had what seemed to be a plausible accident. That's what he told himself it must have been — an accident. But he kept thinking about the tree trunk and the old iron lathe. And he was relieved when they finally started out for home later that afternoon.

Chapter Ten

'What's up?' Jake asked as he came down the steps, on his way out for the day.

David, just returning from Skyline Drive, stared at him and didn't answer.

Jake shrugged, pushed his big hat back on his head, and went out, quietly closing the door behind him.

David went up the stairs to his room. Nobody had noticed he was gone. Nobody was going to ask where he'd been. Or why. Or anything else.

By nobody, he meant Gordon. He was too busy with Mandy to remember that David was alive. Gordon only had time for David when Mandy was out, out shopping, out with a girl friend for a long lunch at Old Ebbitt's or the Jefferson Hotel. Gordon didn't care about him any more. So why did David listen to him?

David didn't understand that himself. He never intended to listen, not since Mandy came into their lives. He never intended to

191

pay any attention to what Gordon said. But he found that he couldn't help himself. It was a habit. It had always been that way. When Gordon talked, David took the words in, and the meaning, and they became *his* words, and *his* meaning. That was how he thought about it. Gordon's words became *his* words.

That was why he'd gone to Big Meadows. That was why he'd followed Elianne when she went out with Hank. He hadn't been close enough to hear what they were saying, but they were together so Gordon was right. And because Gordon was right, David followed Elianne when she went out alone that morning. And, suddenly feeling as strong as a young god, he grabbed the rusty bar that was lying there on the ridge, and set it over the fallen tree trunk, and slid it under that grey rock, and set the whole earth to shaking with one big heave . . .

He hadn't thought about it in advance. He hadn't known he was going to do it. Only Gordon's words were in his mind.

But nobody even knew that he'd been away. The car was back where it belonged. He'd cleaned the dirt off his shoes and the sweat off his face. It was as if nothing had happened. He'd seen Elianne tumble away while the boulder thundered by. He'd seen her rise from the cloud of dust and flee away along the trail, whole and swift. A little later he'd started out for home.

Now he went to the window and peered through the wistaria's thick growth. Gordon and Mandy were coming around the side of the house, walking slowly along the terrace.

'Oh, Gordie,' Mandy said, 'I'm so happy. It's a wonderful surprise.'

Gordon laughed. 'I told you I'd do it, didn't I?'

'You did. You did. And I'm so happy. It's just the colour I wanted. It'll be so much fun.' The car was indeed just what she wanted: a red convertible El Dorado, with white leather upholstery. The licence was in her name. It was tucked into her handbag, and she was determined that there it would stay.

She'd been at him about the car for weeks. Now she had it, it seemed a good time to tell him what else she'd been thinking about. 'You know, Gordie . . . all that money you're going to get when you turn twenty-five?'

'What about it?' He was sorry now that he'd bragged about it. She kept thinking of things she wanted, had to have, and couldn't live without.

'You were saying you couldn't get your hands on it now. Not for anything. But you're wrong about that. You can if you want to.'

'No way,' he said. 'I've already talked to

the lawyer. He wouldn't even discuss it. And I know it's no use trying Elianne. She's as bad as he is. Maybe worse.'

'Never mind them,' Mandy said. 'What do they know?' She squeezed Gordon's arm, but didn't say any more. That was enough for now. Let him wonder a little. 'Let's go for a ride in my new car,' she said instead.

David stepped away from the window, sickness rising in this throat. Mandy's soft syrupy words . . . Gordon's fatuous chuckle. He hated her. He couldn't stand Gordon.

David threw himself on the bed and covered his head with the pillow. But he stayed there for only moments, every muscle in his body thrumming, his pulses banging away beneath the skin of his wrists and throat, and behind his ears like drumbeats.

Then he jumped up. He walked quickly around the room, door to window, window to door. Finally he seized a book on the shelf. He pulled it out and ripped away a handful of pages. He went on tearing out pages until the hardback cover was empty, its spine shredding. Then, taking handfuls of sheets at a time, he ripped them across, then across again, reducing them to tiny pieces that lay like snow across the dark brown carpet.

They were still there the next day when Keith knocked at the door, asked if he could come in and talk to David.

But Keith pretended not to see them when he entered the room at David's invitation. He rolled his wheel chair to the window and turned it around so that the light was behind him. David, sitting on the edge of the bed, had a slanting angle of the setting sun directly on his face.

He squinted a little, his hands on his knees, waiting.

Keith hesitated, not knowing how to begin. He and David had always got along. He and Gordon had always got along too. He didn't want to spoil that. But he knew he had to do something. He had to say something. But there was still a small niggling doubt in him. What had David done? How could he have done it?

He said, 'I was wondering . . . I mean, what have you been doing with yourself?'

David shrugged. 'Hanging around. Hanging out. What else is there to do?'

'With school out, you have the whole summer ahead of you. Maybe you ought to make some plans.'

'Plans?'

'About what you'll do.'

'I guess I'll do the same as always. Why are you asking?'

'Because I've been thinking about you,

David. You're pretty smart, you know it? You should start to look ahead to your future. You should go to college and get a real education. You can go to George Washington, if you like. Like Elianne. Or maybe you'd rather go away. If I could, that's what I'd do.'

'Go away,' David repeated softly. A spark seemed to glow briefly in his eyes. 'Is that your idea or Elianne's?' But he hardly noticed Keith shake his head. Maybe Keith didn't even realize that she had put the idea into his mind. It didn't matter. They had talked about him behind his back. He was sure it was Elianne's idea. Of course it was. She wanted to get rid of him. She wanted to send him away from Hannah's Gate. It was okay for Jake to be here. Okay for Hank. Okay for Keith. And Gordon and Mandy. But not okay for David. David had to leave Hannah's Gate.

'Elianne never said anything about it to me,' Keith was telling him. 'And you don't have to do that anyhow. It was just a thought I had. I was remembering how it was for me . . .' Keith's voice died away. He'd left for Kent State, looking ahead to his future. He'd come back with what might have been his future unalterably changed forever. 'It's an adventure,' he said finally. 'Going away to study.' It was like a dream now for him, as if Kent State had never happened.

David said nothing. He waited. Keith had something on his mind, but he hadn't got to it yet. He would though, if David gave him enough time.

Keith ran his fingers along the arms of the chair. Long fingers, slender and smooth. Strong fingers, strong hands.

David's hands were strong too. He looked down at his bunched fists. He had all the time in the world. He had the rest of his life. He could wait.

At last Keith said softly, 'Hank and Elianne have a right to be happy, David. They have a right to be in love.'

He remembered the tall shadow, the familiar shaped head. Once more he saw it slide into the trees at Big Meadow Lodge. He remembered Elianne's face when she told him, and Hank, about what had happened when she was out walking alone. The tumbling rock . . . the stumble that had saved her . . . He didn't speak of Skyline Drive. But he didn't have to.

As he listened, David's squinting eyes widened. He raised his head. Beyond Keith's silhouette the light in the window was fading fast. The leaves of the wistaria were beginning to look black.

In the face of David's silence, Keith went on slowly, 'They're your friends, David.

197

They're on your side. They only want what's best for you. Just as I do.'

Still David said nothing.

'I wish you were on *their* side. I wish you understood how they feel. Maybe if you tried, you could. I know that one day you will. You'll meet a special girl, and you'll feel just the same. Then you'll know how it is for them now.'

Keith knew that he wasn't saying what he wanted to say. He wasn't making his meaning clear. David's face was as blank as always. It was hard, even, to be sure he was listening.

Keith thought of a tall thin silhouette leaning towards a window . . . A slim moving shadow dodging from tree to tree . . . Spying. Following. Why?

He leaned forward, and said softly, 'Please leave them alone, David. Don't watch them any more. Don't follow them. They need time together.'

David didn't have to think of what he was going to do. It was there. In his mind. The plan formulated, only the when of it left to be decided on. He had no doubts. He had no questions. It was there, ready, in his mind. As if he had been considering it for hours, days. He squinted his eyes and said aloud, 'I don't know what you're talking about, Keith.'

The moon rose slowly over the brick wall

that fronted on to Afton Place. Full and red, wreathed by a faint pinkish mist, it seemed to climb the dark sky on ladders of drifting white clouds.

David looked through the leaves of the wistaria at his window, watching as the moon gained height, and silvered, layering the long slope and unlit pool with ribboned shadows.

Here, in the house, there was darkness too. Irene had gone to watch television in her third-floor room hours before, and now the set was silent, and she was asleep.

Jake was abed in the new wing. His big black hat rode a lamp shade. His dusty black boots were just inside the unlocked door. The stash of pot and cigarette papers, and the assortment of pills, were hidden in his backpack at the back of the cupboard.

David knew about that, about how the room looked, because he had examined both several times. The most recent time had been only two hours ago.

Hank was in his room next door. Keith was in the room beyond that. David was certain of the whereabouts of both men because he had looked in on them too.

Elianne slept alone in the corner room.

The moon rose higher. The shadows lengthened. A small plane buzzed across the horizon, red and white lights blinking, its hum slowly fading as it disappeared into the sky.

The returning silence was thick, muffling. It seemed that the house, the grounds, maybe all the world was empty. It seemed that nothing lived, nothing breathed.

Then a faint stirring whispered in the wistaria leaves. David listened for a moment before he stepped up to the sill and out of the open window. The stirring in the leaves continued as he swung himself, hand over hand, along the vine, his feet in sneakers swift and sure on its rough old limbs. The wistaria creaked and sighed. Its leaves rustled against him, touching his body, his face, his bare arms, like the stroking of silken feathers.

Hand over hand, with only a faint stirring of the leaves, he went from his room, past Hank's and then beyond.

Keith's window was open.

David listened. The rustle of the wistaria stilled. There was no sound from within. There was no light. Soundlessly, David climbed into the room and swiftly crossed the carpeted floor.

Keith lay on his back, high on several pillows. Beside him on a night table there was a bell to be rung if he needed Hank in the night. There was also a glass of water. A book, open and face down. The cut-out of a newspaper picture of the new plane that had just begun to fly from Paris to New York in three hours: the Concorde.

After a long silent moment, staring into Keith's shadowed face, David went to the sofa and took a blue pillow. He returned on silent feet to Keith's bed.

Keith slept on, his face young and unmarked.

David pictured him smiling. He pictured him with that faint shadow of suspicion in his eyes. He pictured Keith staring at him in accusation.

He bent over and pressed the blue pillow firmly over Keith's face.

Chapter Eleven

Hank awakened suddenly with his fists clenched. He had been dreaming. Fragments of his dream still drifted like a dark mist in his mind. A ridge . . . broken earth . . . an iron lathe . . . What had sent the boulder tumbling down to the path where Elianne walked? He opened his eyes. Bright bars of sunlight marked the window. It was day. He was no longer on Skyline Drive but in his bedroom at Hannah's Gate.

He looked at his watch. It was seven-thirty. In a little while, Keith would ring for him.

The uneasiness of the day before still clung to him. As he showered and shaved and dressed, he tried to reason it away. Why would anyone try to hurt Elianne? An iron bar and a tree trunk didn't necessarily add up to an attack on her, did they?

He glanced at his watch again. Now it was almost half-past eight. Keith was sleeping later than usual.

Hank stood at the window, looking down at the pool. Carl Utah was already there, watering some big flower pots. A quiet guy, Carl. Hank found himself wondering about the older man. Where he had come from. What he had done before he came to Hannah's Gate . . .

Hank noticed that the curtains at the cottage windows were still drawn. Gordon and Mandy hadn't risen yet. They were usually late going to bed, and late to rise in the morning. Hank wondered how long this thing between Gordon and Mandy would last. Mandy was plainly restless these days, showing all the signs of a woman bored with her man. Poor Gordon. His infatuation seemed as strong as ever. Hank asked himself what would happen when Mandy decided that she'd extorted all she could, and decided to bail out. Hank didn't know the answer, but he had the feeling that whatever was going to happen would happen soon.

He turned from the window, checking the time again. Now it was nearly nine o'clock. He decided to give Keith another half hour. Perhaps he too hadn't had a good night. He hadn't called Hank, but he might have been wakeful anyway. Hank himself still felt tired. As if, instead of sleeping in his own bed, he had been active all through the night. He supposed it was what was left of his dream. Maybe, after he'd seen Elianne, he'd feel better. She had seemed okay the night before, but still . . .

He got orange juice in the dining room. He looked into the kitchen and found Irene and told her that he and Keith would be down by ten for breakfast. He apologized that they'd be so late, knowing that they'd be interfering with her routine. She told him not to hurry. She'd leave breakfast set up until he and Keith were ready.

At nine-thirty, he went upstairs. He'd planned to take Keith to the National Art Gallery. But if Keith were tired, they'd go another day, he decided. As he passed Elianne's room, he heard her moving around. He went on to Keith's door, listened. It was quiet within. It struck him as odd that Keith hadn't yet rung the bell for him, hadn't turned on the transistor to pick up the morning news, as was his habit. He eased the door open, and knew immediately that something was wrong.

The room was dark, except for the bright square of the window. He crossed the space in two long strides, the heavy empty silence enfolding him, his breath caught in his throat, his pulses racing.

Keith lay on his stomach, his face pressed

into the white pillow, another white pillow covering his head. The square blue pillow was back on the sofa now, where it belonged, so Hank didn't even see it, as he whispered, 'Oh, God, no!'

He touched Keith's shoulder, his cheek. Cold. Cold. 'Keith! No!'

Silence.

Hank grabbed the telephone, dialed 911, gave the address of Hannah's Gate, and cried, 'Hurry! Hurry! We need help fast!' Then he dropped the telephone and ran into the hall. Elianne! He would have to tell her. He tapped at her door, flung it open. 'Elianne! Something's wrong!'

She came towards him, her arms out, her face paling. 'Hank! What?'

'It's Keith,' Hank said. 'I've called an ambulance!'

He hurried back to Keith's room, Elianne on his heels.

She sank to her knees beside the bed, catching Keith's limp hand in hers. She looked up at Hank. 'Is he . . . is he . . . ?'

Hank didn't answer her. He put a hand on her shoulder.

But she already knew. She bent her head. Tears spilled from her eyes, ran down her cheeks, fell on Keith's cold hand. She knew that he was dead.

The medical examiner said that Keith had died by suffocation. The autopsy agreed with his opinion. Hank's description of how Keith's body had been lying when he first entered the room that morning was consistent with that finding. Everyone agreed that Keith had suffered a terrible accident. Somehow he had turned his face into the pillow, and, unable to move, had died.

Hank remembered Keith's very strong arms. If he'd managed to turn himself over, he should have been able to turn himself on to his back again. Repeatedly, Hank pictured the scene in his mind: the window open, light streaming in. The bedroom area of the room dark with shadows. The bedcovers smooth. Only the two white pillows crumpled, one beneath Keith's face, the other wedged along the side of his head. Keith's body on his stomach, his face buried. Repeatedly Hank pictured it, and it always looked wrong to him. Keith shouldn't have been able to get himself rolled over on his stomach. In all the years Hank had been with him, Keith hadn't been able to do that. And if, somehow, he had, then his strong arms ought to have been able to shift himself back. It was wrong, Hank told himself. But he had no explanation for what had happened so he didn't voice his doubts.

It was the same for Elianne. She couldn't accept the way Keith had died. It didn't make sense to her. She moved dully through the first few days after his death. She made the arrangements for his funeral, with Hank's help. She went to the funeral with the rest of the family. With Gordon and David. With Hank and Jack and Carl and Irene. All the while, the questions echoed in her mind. What had happened? Why had Keith died? How had he died?

Several days after his burial, she read his obituary in the Washington *Post*. It said that Keith Devlin, twenty-five-year-old former student at Kent State, who had been crippled as a result of wounds received during the anti-Vietnam war riots of 1970 there, had died unexpectedly in his Cleveland Park home.

That same morning, Carrie Day read the same obituary and made a few quick notes to herself before she went on to finish one more chapter of her autobiography. She didn't know why she bothered to do it. In her time Washington had seen a lot worse than a senator's having an illegitimate daughter. Still, maybe there'd be somebody left who cared. With the chapter done, she took up the notes she had made about Keith Devlin, and then put in a call to the woman she knew at the Washington *Times*.

207

The following week a full column in the *Times* was devoted to the unexpected death of Keith Devlin. This time he was described as a scion of the Gowan, Loving, Merrill families, the son of Rea Loving Devlin, who had died years before when abandoned by her beatnik lover in Mexico. It also mentioned the dark history of Hannah's Gate, and the murders that had occurred there in the 1940s.

Elianne read those words uneasily. Hannah's Gate . . . its dark history. Margo Desales. Linda Grant. The other deaths . . . her father and mother . . . her grandmother . . . her Uncle Brett . . . And now, now Keith. Keith, who was so young . . . just a few years older than she was.

She tried not to dwell on it, but questions lingered in her mind. What had happened to Keith? Why had he died? How had he died? She wanted to ask if Hank had heard anything, if David had. But it seemed awkward. Wouldn't they have spoken up if they'd heard anything? Wouldn't they speak up now if they had any reason to doubt what everyone thought had happened to Keith?

Two weeks later, Foster Talcott called. After asking how she was, he said, 'I have business to discuss, Elianne. You do, of course, remember that four trusts were set up in your

208

mother's will? Do you recall that if any one of you died, you, Gordon, David, or Keith, the remaining three are to share the principal of that trust?'

She was startled when the lawyer spoke of that provision. She had forgotten it entirely. It hadn't occurred to her that anyone would benefit from Keith's death. She waited for Talcott to continue. But even then she asked herself if his trust had had anything to do with Keith's death? Had someone, somehow, managed to kill Keith and make his suffocation appear accidental? Did she dare even think it? Had murder come to Hannah's Gate again?

A swift chill touched her. Keith's death *must* have been an accident. But the day before, at Skyline Drive, there had been another accident. Was it coincidence that a boulder had tumbled down from the ridge above the path where she was walking?

The lawyer was saying, 'Accordingly, each one of you surviving will now have a larger trust.'

'I see,' she said, her voice a dry whisper.

'The yearly incomes will increase. You'll have to decide what to do about the allowances given to Gordon and David. And to yourself, of course.'

'Whatever you suggest,' she said.

'I'll consider it and be back in touch with

you. Meanwhile, is there anything I can do?' ˉ

She hesitated, thinking about Keith's death, her doubts and fears. How could she explain to him? What could she ask him to do? At last she said, 'There's nothing now.'

'If anything should come up . . .'

'Thank you,' she said. And: 'I'll expect to hear from you.'

It was another two weeks before she heard from him again. Then he telephoned. She suggested he come to Hannah's Gate the following afternoon.

When he arrived, she was reading a calendar of events for the Fourth of July celebration to be held the following day on the mall. It was combined with a series of Bicentennial events.

Just six weeks before, Keith had expressed interest in attending some of the Bicentennial ceremonies, and Hank had assured him that they would. But six weeks ago, Hank hadn't known that Keith would now be dead, Elianne thought.

She quickly flipped the pages back to the first one. There was a headline: Israelis had made a daring raid on an airport in Entebbe.

The lawyer, looking over her shoulder, said, 'A lot is happening these days.'

She put the paper aside, nodding soberly.

'To business then.' Talcott wore a light

brown bowtie that afternoon. His eyes were solemn behind his heavy glasses. He gave her a small document. 'These are my recommendations for the three allowances. The figures at the bottom indicate the principal in the trusts before Keith's share is added to them, and the second set of figures indicates what there will be when his share is added. Do you understand?' At her nod, he continued, 'But there's something else. It's come up within the past two weeks. It has taken me some time to investigate it. I needed to know where we stood before discussing it with you.

'A while ago I received an unofficial phone call from an acquaintance of mine in the Office of the Registrar of Wills. It's where all wills in the District of Columbia are filed for probate. My caller informed me that an attorney had sought to read your mother's will. I had never heard of the man, but I decided to ask him what his interest was. He refused to disclose it then, but offered to come to see me. I agreed. The next day he appeared at my office. I didn't care for his looks, I can tell you. After some to-ing and fro-ing, he said that he represented a client who had an interest in your mother's will. When I asked what interest, this person wouldn't explain. I decided to find out who his client was.' Talcott smiled grimly. 'As you probably know, I am not without influence in this city. This person got the idea that if he were to reveal to me the name of his client, he would end up with many more clients than he has now, clients of a more remunerative sort. So he gave me his client's name.' Talcott paused.

'And who is it?' Elianne asked, impatient with Talcott's pomposity. 'What does he have to do with any of us?'

'The man's name is John Reedy. He is quite well known, as an entrepreneur and money lender, in Georgetown. A man of poor reputation but substantial wealth, I'm told. Have you ever heard of him?'

'No. Never. I can't imagine . . .'

Talcott cut in, 'I have not been told, but I suspect that Gordon has been to see John Reedy. That Gordon intends to borrow from him on his share of his coming inheritance.'

'Oh, no,' Elianne whispered.

'It's what I suspect.'

'What can I do?'

'I believe you must confront him, Elianne.'

'I wouldn't know what to say.'

'The gist of it must be that if Gordon becomes involved in such an arrangement, you will ask me to go to court to have him declared incompetent. I believe that will stop him.'

A chill crept over her body. She could feel the slow frightened pounding of her heart.

'He mustn't be allowed to get involved with John Reedy,' Talcott said. 'You must prevent it, Elianne.'

Later, when she was alone, she went over it in her mind. Keith's share would be divided between all three of them. She would have to increase David and Gordon's allowances. And somehow she would have to tell Gordon that Foster Talcott had told her about John Reedy. Then she would have to invoke the threat that the lawyer proposed. Did she dare? Could she? What would Gordon say?

From outside she heard the beat of rock and roll, the shrill sound of Mandy's laughter.

Elianne listened, remembering what Talcott had told her. She would have to do what he said, she knew. But not now. Not yet. She couldn't deal with it yet.

Mandy was at the pool. She wore high-heeled red sandals, a tiny red bra top, and small red briefs. Her body was silky and smooth, evenly tanned. Her red hair flowed like liquid fire on her shoulders. Her long slim legs flashed as she spun and swayed to the sound of the music from the transistor. She pranced up to David, seized him by the hand. 'Come on, baby. Let's show them how to do it,' she cried, her smile gleaming.

'Let go of me,' David yelled, stepping back

as if her touch burned him. 'I can't dance.'

'Come on, sweetness,' she crooned. 'I'll teach you. It's easy.'

But he stamped away, his shoulders rigid.

'Guess he doesn't want to,' Mandy laughed, smiling at Jake. She put her arms out. 'How about you? You can do it, can't you?'

His teeth flashed in his beard. 'Maybe. If I remember.' He put his wide-brimmed hat on a beach chair and stepped close to her, close but not touching. His hips swayed. His shoulders rolled. Not touching, the two of them mirrored each other's movements. 'I didn't know I still had it in me,' Jake said.

'Oh, yes, you do,' Mandy purred. She shot a glance at the chair where Gordon sat, glaring at her from beneath lowered lids. 'Seems like I've been wrong about you, Jake.'

'Wrong?'

'I thought you were crazy. Now I'm beginning to think there's something going on behind all the hair on your face.'

'There's something going on,' Jake assured her.

Gordon yelled, 'Mandy! If you want to go shopping, we've got to get going.'

Mandy said swiftly, 'Listen, Jake, you and me — we ought to get together. We've got a lot to talk about, haven't we?'

'My love is divine,' Jake told her, smiling.

'I'll bet it is,' she retorted. She started towards the cottage to change into street clothes.
As she passed Carl Utah, who was fertilizing
a weigela bush, she blew him a quick kiss.

Inside the cottage, Gordon demanded,
'What did you have to dance with that freak
for?'

'I felt like it,' she said.

'Well, quit feeling like it. I don't trust him.
I want him out of here.'

'He's kind of interesting,' she said. 'I'll bet
he knows a thing or two.'

'Knows what?'

'I can't tell you that. Maybe everything. He
has his eyes open. Haven't you noticed?'

Gordon didn't say anything more, but he
kept thinking about her words. Jake, doing
nothing, always just hanging around. Jake,
with his eyes wide open. Wise Jake was seeing
too much of Mandy, that's what he was seeing.
And maybe he was more than seeing. Gordon
knew he couldn't tell about Mandy. It made
him sick to think of it. Mandy, grabbing at
David, swinging herself at Jake, at old Carl
Utah too. It made Gordon so mad that he
couldn't stop thinking about it all afternoon.

That night he asked David to come down
to the cottage.

Mandy was in the bedroom, doing her nails.

Gordon and David were alone together. It

felt to David like it had before — before Mandy came to Hannah's Gate. Gordon and David . . . Just the two of them. But it wasn't the same. Because Mandy was just the other side of the wall. David sensed her presence, smelled her perfume, remembered the sting of her touch.

Gordon said quietly, 'Damn! I miss Keith. I really do. It's too bad about him, isn't it?'

David was instantly alert. Keith. Why was Gordon speaking of Keith now? It was six weeks since he'd picked up the blue sofa pillow . . .

Gordon went on, 'It shouldn't have happened to him. It should have been Jake Babbitt. That guy's a phoney and a freak. I have the feeling that he's after Elianne. And one of these days, he's going to make big trouble for us.'

David looked into Gordon's face, said nothing.

Gordon nodded. 'Believe me, I know. He's getting himself set with Elianne. Why else would he hang around here, doing nothing. Standing against the wall, watching, smiling. And preaching his crazy line.'

David broke into a wide grin. 'Love is divine,' he cried, imitating Jake.

For a moment it really was just the way it used to be between David and Gordon, the two of them smiling at each other.

Then Mandy called from the bedroom, 'Gordie, fix us a drink, will you?'

That was when David left.

Later Mandy and Gordon stopped at the place where they had met. They chatted with the bartender. After a while he remembered that John Reedy had left something for them.

Gordon put it in his jacket pocket. That night, after he and Mandy had made love, he took it out and read it. It looked all right to him. But he couldn't find a pen. He decided to sign it in the morning, and went to bed.

Chapter Twelve

Jake hauled his backpack from the corner of the cupboard. He looked inside: a couple of dog-eared paperbacks; socks with holes at toe and heel; strings of beans and acorns, their natural dyes faded. There were two shirts hanging on the rack. A single pair of trousers. A set of ragged tennis shoes. It wasn't much for a man who was turning thirty-seven that month of October.

All the places he'd been . . . he pictured a map in his mind. The states where Jake Babbitt had stopped, or passed through, were coloured red. Nearly every state was. Not Hawaii, not Alaska, but nearly all the rest. He saw the yellow sun of Mississippi, simmering through the hot humid air. He imagined the clear golden sun of New Mexico scalding the dry mesa wind. In Mississippi, the Freedom Riders, and Goodman, Chaney and Schwerner. In New Mexico, Love City and Elianne.

The things he'd seen. The bright-coloured

dreams. He unwrapped the stash of pills, ran his fingers lightly over them. LSD. Acid. He didn't want it. He didn't need it. He re-wrapped the pills, thrust them back into the pack. He took out paper and the envelope of brown leaves. He rolled a joint, lit up, and sat back, letting the smoke burn through him.

The quiet room was soothing. Hannah's Gate was a good crash pad, and he'd managed to string out his stay. But the place was full of bad vibes. They'd grown worse since Keith died. Jake's stomach quivered at the thought. Something wrong there. But no, it had nothing to do with him. He wasn't going to think about it. Still, he missed Keith, the squeak of his wheel chair, the hum of the lift cage. But bad vibes, yes. He'd felt them right away. Jake Babbitt was sensitive to bad vibes. He'd come here, he knew now, because of Elianne, hoping for something, although he wasn't sure what. Whatever he'd hoped was useless. Elianne had drifted away from him when she tried to stop being Ella Em. So it was time for him to go on.

But first he had to think. To think . . . that was it. He didn't know it, but he was in the process of re-inventing himself. He was digging for a new Jake Babbitt, searching for him deep inside.

The joint burned down. He stubbed out the

roach, and considered lighting another. But he let it go. He used to think that marijuana gave him the key that opened many doors within his mind. Now, though, he only felt slowed down, empty. He saw that he had nothing to show for all the years, the states he'd been through, the people he'd known. It was time now to think of a new way. What did he want? What was he good for? Who the hell was he?

Later he went downstairs, out to the terrace, and then down to the pool, where Carl Utah was getting it ready for winter. He had carried three good-sized logs from the woodpile to the pool's edge. The logs, he told Jake, would prevent damage to the concrete walls when the water froze. He assured Jake it was better to do this than to empty the pool. Then with Jake helping, Carl pulled a heavy blue tarpaulin over the pool, and secured it at all four corners.

From there, Carl went on to another autumn chore. Jake followed, watched him delicately pluck dead flowers from the rose bushes.

When Carl looked up, Jake said, 'You like flowers.'

'Growing things. Living things. You get a satisfaction, handling them,' Carl told him.

'Your soul gets satisfaction,' Jake said.

Carl didn't answer, but he shot Jake a quick

questioning look.

'Yes,' Jake said. 'That's why you do it. It's why you like it.' He paused, letting the thought come to him. He too needed satisfaction for his soul. He could learn anything. He knew that about himself. He asked, 'Did you ever think about having a business? I mean, like growing flowers, selling them?'

'I never did.'

'Begin to think about it now.' Jake hurried on, pushed by the ideas suddenly crowding in on him: 'A small place. You and me. You doing the flowers because you know about that. Arrangements. Centrepieces. The stuff you like to do. Me doing the business end. Because I know about that. Selling to people.' He nodded, grinning. 'Yes, that's what I know. How to sell to people.'

Carl took his time before responding. He wondered what this guy Jake was after. There was something peculiar about him. But Carl figured that there was something peculiar about just about everybody in Hannah's Gate. He wouldn't give a plugged nickel for any one of them. Except Elianne. He thought she was special. But he wished she was happy, the way a girl her age ought to be. Happy. In love. Planning her future. That was how it should be for Elianne. Only it wasn't. And things had worsened since Keith's death.

Jake coughed loudly. 'What do you think, Carl?'

'I don't know what to think. It takes money to open up a business, and that's something I never had. Money.' He turned slowly, taking in the house behind, then swinging to look beyond the terraces at the pool, the cottage. All the money was with the Lovings, the Washington family, here at Hannah's Gate. None was with the Utah branch, in New Mexico.

'We could figure it out,' Jake said. 'There's those small business loans the government will give you. We can check up on them.'

'I don't know where to start,' Carl answered, spreading his hands. 'I only know about gardening and building.'

'All you've got to do is ask until you get the right person,' Jake nodded. 'Let me think about it.' And he wandered away.

It had taken a long time for Elianne to nerve herself to talk to Gordon. Talcott had called twice to ask if she had done it, sounding more disapproving each time she had said she was still trying to decide what to do. But finally, on a bright afternoon in mid-October, she and Gordon retired to the study alone, at her suggestion.

Gordon slouched on the sofa under the portrait of Big Jack Gowan. His head was back, his legs outspread. His full face was flushed. He knew why she had summoned him. At least he thought he did. He was tired of being treated like a kid. He was Gordon Merrill, of Hannah's Gate, and he was going to make sure that she didn't forget it. He said truculently, 'Okay, Elianne. I'm here. And I'm alone. Now what do you want?'

She twisted her hands together and held them in her lap to keep them from trembling. She said, 'Gordon, Mr Talcott tells me that he has reason to believe that you've involved yourself with a very unsavoury person named John Reedy.'

Gordon laughed. 'If you only knew what you sound like . . .'

'I don't care how I sound.' She drew a deep breath. 'Mr Talcott says you either intend to, or have already, borrowed on your future inheritance.'

'What of it?' Actually Gordon was worried about what had been happening. It was a long while since he'd signed the damned papers Reedy wanted signed, and dropped them off, and he'd heard nothing. When he tried to reach Reedy directly, he couldn't find him. So Gordon was beginning to worry about what was going on. But he didn't see why Elianne had to know that.

She was saying, 'It won't do for you to deal with John Reedy, Gordon. It'll be five years before you receive your share of the money. Meanwhile you'll be paying more interest than you imagine.' These were Foster Talcott's arguments. She was just repeating them as he had given them to her.

'Let me worry about that,' Gordon retorted. 'I know what I'm doing.'

'I don't think that you do. Neither does Mr Talcott. He says . . .' She paused, took a deep breath, 'He says that if I give him permission to act, he will. You are still under age. He feels he can break any contract backed up only by your signature.'

'What?' Gordon said hoarsely.

'There's more,' she cut in quickly. 'He said if it proves to be necessary he'll go to court to request that you be declared incompetent to make financial transactions.'

Gordon went rigid. He rose half way from the sofa, then let himself drop back. 'That's crazy!'

'It can be done, Gordon. If we show the court the money you've spent . . .'

He no longer cared about honey and vinegar and Mandy's advice. He was so angry he had to explode. He demanded, 'Who do you think you are? What gives you the right to decide for me what I do, or how and when I spend my money. *My* money, damn you!'

'Gordon . . .'

'Shut up,' he shouted. 'I'm tired of your lectures. I'm tired of you. I'm a grown man. *I* should be running Hannah's Gate. And I would be — except for you.'

'I can't help that. I only want to do what's best for you.'

'Let me tell you,' he said through his teeth. 'Let me tell you to think about it, long and hard, before you do anything. And tell Foster Talcott to think about it too. You're not in any position to make any complaints to any goddamn court about me. How could you be? You've got Jake Babbitt living in this house. A nut. A freak. Anybody looking at him, listening to him, could tell that. And he's living here, off us. You talk about Mandy, and I'm going to talk about Jake.'

'You know that's different,' Elianne said.

'I don't know it's different,' Gordon retorted. 'And there's the little matter of Hank too. Keith's dead. Hank's job is done. Why is he still hanging around?' Gordon got up, went to the door. 'So watch what you do, damn it! Because you might start something you can't finish.'

He told himself that nothing was going to stop him. He needed money, and now, and he was going to get it. But that night he learned that John Reedy didn't want to do business with him after all. He sent word to Gordon that the agreement had been destroyed. Somebody had been asking questions. John Reedy didn't consider him a good risk any more.

Mandy had gone out. Gordon didn't know where. He'd been angry about it before but now he was glad she wasn't there. He had two very stiff drinks, and went up to the house to talk to David.

Chapter Thirteen

The conversation at dinner was about the presidential election that was coming up at the beginning of the following week. Then Mandy spoke about the fashion show she had seen at Neiman Marcus that afternoon, and Gordon spoke of getting tickets to a Redskins' game.

Jake, who rarely turned up to eat with the rest of them, usually preferring to scrounge a sandwich in the kitchen from Irene, came in at the last minute, taking Hank's unoccupied place.

Hank arrived after Irene had served the first course. She brought him a place setting, and a crab cocktail, so he could catch up.

He apologized for being late, explaining that he'd been delayed downtown at the hospital, talking to Amy Carroll. Charlie had had a heart attack two days before. He was going to be all right, but the recovery would take some time.

Elianne told Hank she was sorry about

Charlie, then lapsed into silence. She was thinking of Keith. He had been dead for four months now. She missed him constantly. Until he was gone, she hadn't realized how much she had depended on him. They had had, between them, the closeness she had always wished for with her brothers. Wished for, and never known. As her glance touched Gordon and David, moved on to Mandy, and then to Jake, she thought that an outsider might be fooled for a little while into thinking that here sat a family with several friends. People linked together by blood and love, and by feeling in common. How wrong that would be. There were bonds between them, but hardly of love. And the only thing they had in common was Hannah's Gate.

It was terrible to feel so alone. She shivered, drew her blue shawl more closely around her throat. The chill of autumn seemed to seep through the windows, to blow along the carpeted floor. She could feel Hank's gaze touch her, but resolutely avoided looking at him. No. She must forget how it had been to cling to him, to taste his lips. No. There was nothing between them any more. That was how it had to be. She didn't know what love was. Maybe she had never known.

The conversation had died. David was as quiet as usual. Now Gordon concentrated on eating the roast beef Irene had just brought in. Gordon had apologized to her for exploding when she had tried to talk to him about borrowing money against his trust fund. 'I just lost my head,' he'd said. 'I shouldn't have. I know you meant it for the best, Elianne.'

But she had wondered what he was thinking about behind his strained smile. She didn't know, of course, that the deal had fallen through anyhow.

Over dessert, Jake suggested going to Georgetown that night. 'There's a good guitarist playing down the road from Blue's Alley.' He was looking at Elianne. 'How about coming?' The invitation plainly didn't extend to the others.

Elianne hesitated. She wasn't sure she wanted to go out with Jake, but the idea of going out appealed to her.

Then Hank said, 'It's a good idea.' And with a grin at Jake, 'I'll come too.' He turned to look at Elianne, as if daring her to agree.

'There'll be Hallowe'en crowds,' she said doubtfully. 'But okay. Let's see what it's like.'

Jake chuckled, pleased with himself. He was feeling good. Everyone had had something to say about his having shaved off his beard, but now they were used to it. He was getting used to it too.

As they were finishing the meal, Gordon

set his cup down with a sharp click. He leaned back in his chair and fixed his eyes on Hank. 'I've been meaning to ask you . . . what are your plans?'

'My plans?' Hank repeated.

'What you intend to do,' Gordon went on. 'Now that Keith is dead, we don't need a companion for him, do we? So you don't have a job here any more. When do you expect to leave?'

'Hank doesn't answer to you.' Elianne said gently. Unconsciously her hands went to her hair. She smoothed it back from her forehead, settled it behind her ears with a quick flip. Gordon's brows rose. 'I'm sorry, Elianne. But I pay part of Hank's salary with my money, don't I? That gives me the right to ask how long that's going to go on.'

For a moment she was speechless, assailed by sudden anguish. Finally she had to face the possibility of Hank's leaving Hannah's Gate. Since Keith's death, she had managed to avoid thinking about it. That was no longer avoidable. She had to realize that soon Hank would leave. She would never see him again. It was an unbearable thought. Yet that recognition was followed instantly by confusion. What did she expect? What did she want? She'd broken off their affair, hadn't she? She had refused to consider marrying him, hadn't she? Then what difference did it make to her whether he stayed or went. But it *did* make a difference. Even if she didn't know why.

Hank said quietly, 'I thought you knew, Gordon. I haven't accepted a salary since Keith's death.'

Gordon looked at Elianne for confirmation.

'Yes,' she said quietly. 'It's true. I should have told you, Gordon. I'm sorry. You've never been interested in the running of the house so I didn't think it would matter. But now you owe Hank an apology. You've forgotten he's our friend too. And he must stay here with us at Hannah's Gate for as long as he likes.'

Gordon's eyes were sunken, expressionless. He said, 'I'm sorry, Hank. I didn't know . . .'

'It's okay,' Hank said quickly. 'It doesn't matter. But you're right, of course. I've been trying to decide what to do. Now, though, with Charlie Carroll sick, I'll be going to his office to help out. After that . . .' He paused, looked at Elianne. 'We'll see.'

The subject was dropped, much to Hank's relief. He didn't intend to let Gordon drive him away from Hannah's Gate. Never mind what Gordon thought or said: Elianne came first. The uneasiness Hank had felt just before Keith's death persisted. What had really happened on Skyline Drive? What had appeared to be an accident could have been a deliberate attempt to hurt or even kill her. He couldn't ignore the presence of the iron bar and the tree trunk on the ridge. Maybe his vague suspicions were groundless. But the near-miss in the mountains, followed immediately by Keith's death, weighed on Hank.

In the hours immediately after Keith and Elianne and Hank had returned from their weekend trip, he had tried to find out if anyone at Hannah's Gate had been away. After casual questioning of Carl, Jake and Irene, he'd decided that he couldn't be sure. Carl thought he'd seen David and Gordon and Mandy at one time or another all weekend. Jake had said he'd been in and out, and had run into David and Gordon, with Mandy, mornings and evenings. Irene grumbled that she couldn't keep up with the comings and goings of any of them, and didn't try to any more.

So Hank's vague suspicions continued. What was wrong at Hannah's Gate? What did it mean for Elianne? He was sure of nothing. Not even whether he still had a chance with her. But until he was sure, one way or another, he wasn't going to leave.

He had saved most of what he'd earned since he'd begun work as Keith's companion.

There'd been little to spend it on. He had a substantial nest egg, a part of it well invested through Foster Talcott. He could manage without taking salary from Elianne. He would even pay room and board so that he could remain at Hannah's Gate without being uncomfortable about it.

He was about to tell Gordon then and there that he intended to pay for his accommodation in the house until he knew what his plans were, but Mandy said, 'Gordie, come on, will you? We're going to miss the show if you don't get a move on.'

Gordon and Mandy left the table, with David right behind them.

An hour later Hank and Jake and Elianne drove down to Georgetown. They parked near the freeway on K Street after some searching for an open spot. When they walked north, beyond the canal, the streets became crowded with holiday revellers.

Mobs of masked people moved along the pavements, jammed the intersections. There were many rubber-faced Nixons with jutting jaws, heavy black brows and fleshy noses, quite a few witches with hooked beaks and long straggly hair. Devils. Ghosts. Skeletons. Draculas. Indians. Gypsies. Pirates. And policemen. Real policemen, walking in twos, and bunching around squad cars at every corner.

Jake paused before a small empty shop. He peered past the dirty glass. 'See. You could put a nice little business in here.'

'A business?' Elianne echoed. What was he talking about? Jake? Business?

He rubbed his clean-shaven jaw. 'A flower shop maybe.'

'High rent,' Hank said.

'Maybe. Maybe not. The place is really a mess.' Jake pressed his face closer to the glass. 'But it could be fixed up cheaply, with a little paint and soap and water.'

He drew away. No use talking to them about it. He'd have to find how you asked for loans, who you went to. Somebody would know. He intended to learn.

They pushed through the crowds to a lane just south of M Street. Jake led them past Blue's Alley to a smaller club further along.

Inside it was dark, the air thick with cigarette smoke. The music was good. Later a singer came on, all her songs dating from the sixties.

Elianne, listening, thought that the lyrics were written in the words of a foreign language. They belonged to another time, another place. To a girl named Ella Em. She kept her eyes fixed on the small stage, aware of Hank's gaze, aware of his proximity, but refusing to acknowledge either.

For a little while Jake hummed along with the music. Then he said, 'Remember, Elianne?'

'Just barely,' she answered. But it wasn't true. She remembered more, in greater detail, than she wanted to. Love City. Jake whispering, 'I am love. Love is divine.' The sun rising through the eastern sky and descending on the hump of the mountain . . . There were times when she didn't remember. But tonight, here, it all came back. Ella Em came back. Maybe it was the young people, the costumes, the noise and laughter. Maybe it was her mood.

Jake was grinning at her. 'I barely remember too, Elianne.' There was significance in that twist of his lips. He was reminding her that his memory was fogged by the pot he'd smoked and the pills he'd popped, and suggesting that it must be the same for her.

She didn't want to believe it. She hoped it wasn't true. She told herself that she didn't remember the past because it was gone, dead. Ella Em was dead.

Hank said softly, 'Instead of trying to forget it, maybe you should face up to it, deal with it. And accept it.'

Elianne didn't want to listen. She felt as if a sudden weight had dropped from the ceiling, crushing her. A sudden airlessness was choking her. She stumbled to her feet. 'Be right back,' she said. She had to get away from Hank, to be by herself for a little while. She looked around desperately, seeking the lavatory. A waitress directed her to a door opening covered with a curtain of sparkling red, blue and green glass beads.

She thrust it aside and stepped into a long dark corridor. At the end of it, around a corner, she found the ladies' room. The men's room faced it across the narrow hallway. She heard the distant tinkle of glass beads, the whisper of footsteps, as she closed the door behind her.

She washed her face, powdered her nose, and quickly ran her fingers through her hair. There, that was better. She tried not to think of Hank's words. But they were in her mind. She couldn't evade them. *Face up to it, deal with it. And accept it.* Easy for him to say. But he didn't know what it was like. How terrible it could be. Terrible to remember. He didn't know about Ella Em. And suppose he did? What would he think of her then? She could picture him turning away from her in disgust. But it didn't matter, she told herself. Nothing that he might feel about her could matter. She was nothing to Hank any more. He was nothing to her.

A shiver stroked her body. That was easy to say too. But when she thought of him leaving Hannah's Gate for good, it felt as if a piece of her had been torn away. She leaned against the wall, squeezing her eyes shut against a sudden surge of tears. What was happening to her? When had it begun? What should she do? What could she do?

When, finally, she emerged from the lavatory, the corridor was empty. The men's room door opened slightly, but closed again as she passed and turned the corner. She was midway along the hall, hearing the music and voices, when she became aware of a soft sound behind her.

Just that, at first: a soft sound. Then something hit her hard between the shoulders. A quick thrusting jolt. She staggered, slammed into the wall. A muted scream burst from her as an arm encircled her throat, dragging her towards the floor. She had a quick blurred impression of a devil's face, long red tongue thrusting at her, glittering eyes, a snarling, blood-smeared mouth. She fell hard, her arms folded under her, her legs kicking out, the weight between her shoulders increasing. Then, suddenly, she was free.

Out of the dimness came Jake's voice, yelling, 'Hey! What's going on here?'

There was a burst of noise. The bead curtain rattled. Jake's footsteps thumped along the floor. A door around the corner slammed. The music was louder now, and with it, there came a wave of applause, a chorus of approving shouts.

Jake leaned down and pulled Elianne to her feet. She and he were alone in the hallway. Ahead of her, the beaded curtain still swayed. Someone had grabbed her, choked her, thrown her down. And when Jake had come in, that someone had run away.

Jake kept saying, 'Are you all right? Who was that? What happened?'

She smoothed her hair away from her face. She straightened her blouse, and pulled her shawl around her. 'I don't know what happened, Jake. It was a devil. I mean, a devil's mask. That's all I know.'

Jake said he'd been coming in to go to the men's room. There had been a noise. He'd heard her cry out, and stumble forward and fall. He'd seen a shadow duck away.

Now he went to look in the men's room. There was no one inside, but an open window faced an alley. Three or four people were walking by when he looked out. He didn't recognize any of them.

When he returned to Elianne, he asked again, 'You're sure you're all right?' His voice was unsteady. He wrapped his big hands around hers. 'You know, for just a second, when I saw you going down like that, I thought . . . oh God, I thought you were dead, Elianne. Like Keith . . .'

They stared at each other for a long silent moment. Then, surprising herself, she said, 'You're changing, Jake.'

'I am?'

'You hardly ever talk your religion any more. Have you given up believing in it?'

'It's different,' he said.

'But you used to believe in it.'

'Yes, I *did* used to. But, like I say, it feels different now.'

She nodded, and went through the beaded curtain back to Hank.

Jake's voice was still unsteady when he told Hank what had happened. 'Maybe somebody trying to get her bag.' he said. But he was wondering.

Elianne agreed that that was probably it. But she was wondering too.

A little later, David stopped at a dustbin, dropped into it a devil's mask. Then he went into the bar that Mandy used to work in. He took a seat, and tried to catch his breath. He felt as if he'd had a near miss. He felt as if he'd run for miles instead of only a block. He wanted something, but he didn't know what. Finally he ordered a whisky.

The bartender was new. He looked hard

at David. 'I'll need to see an ID,' he said, and added, 'Sir.'

David handed it over. He was used to being asked for it. It didn't make him nervous any more. It had always worked before. He guessed it would work now.

The bartender gave the fake ID back to him. 'Seems like people are getting younger every year,' he said. He grinned, 'Or maybe I'm just getting older.'

David gave him a blank look and slumped on the stool, finally catching his breath.

Thinking back over what had happened, Elianne felt a flutter of fear in her chest. Maybe it was another simple coincidence. Someone trying to steal her bag, as Jake had suggested. But maybe it was something else. It *could* fit into a pattern. The sudden landslide at Skyline Drive . . . her continuing doubts about Keith . . . and now, this evening . . .

Suddenly she wondered if Hank had seen anyone follow her into the corridor. She supposed he hadn't. He'd said nothing about it. She decided she would ask him when the opportunity arose.

When Jake thought about what had happened later, the thing that stuck out in his mind was his own reaction. He'd been overwhelmed by his fear for Elianne. Overwhelmed by despair that something terrible had happened to her. Now, suddenly, he understood why he had come to Hannah's Gate to see Elianne, to see his Ella Em. He'd thought it a whim. He'd had no special place to go, no special thing to do. Ella Em was in Washington. Why not go and see her? Now he understood. He'd been drawn to her because something had remained unfinished between them. At least it had remained unfinished for him. For her, he knew with absolutely certainty, it was completely done. It had been since she fled Taos, and came home. Maybe even before that.

He told himself that it was no use. It was time to push on. But he knew that he wouldn't. Not just yet. He had to remain a little longer in Hannah's Gate.

Mandy and Gordon were in the cottage. The radio was playing. Gordon had been drinking steadily since after dinner. Drinking, and brooding, and muttering under his breath.

While pretending to do her nails, then to read a magazine, Mandy had watched him. Now, tossing the magazine aside, she said, 'That's not going to help, Gordie.'

'Hank's staying around because of Elianne, and for what he can get out of her. I know

241

that. He knows that. We all know that,' Gordon said sourly.

'Okay. So what? You're probably right. But I'm not as absolutely sure as you are. I think something's going on we don't know about. I don't know what exactly.' She got up, paced the room. 'I wish I did know.'

'What are you talking about, Mandy?'

She went and got a small bottle of nail polish and settled down with it, delicately working over her fingertips with the tiny brush. She said after a while, not looking at Gordon, 'I'll tell you . . . in words of one syllable. They don't act the way you'd expect them to act. I'm not sure what's going on any more. He's crazy about her — I can see that in his eyes when he looks at her. And sometimes I think she's crazy about him. But . . . but . . . it's just not quite right.'

'So . . . ?'

'So I'm saying that you shouldn't jump to conclusions. Not until you know for sure.' Mandy waved her hands in the air, drying her newly painted nails. They glistened, a sharp blood red.

'Listen, Mandy, I should own Hannah's Gate and everything else, I know that much. I should own it all. Not Elianne. It's what my father wanted. He knew what she was. He had her all figured out when she was fifteen

242

years old, and she proved that he was completely right about her. But my mother . . .'
Gordon stopped at the knock on the door.

Mandy opened it. David came in.

He stopped just inside, his hands hanging at his sides, clenching and unclenching. His eyes were fixed on Gordon's angry face.

Gordon poured a fresh belt of whisky into a glass, turned to glower at David. 'What are you staring at me for?'

David shrugged.

'Well, damn it, don't look at me like that! I've done the best I could. We're going to end up losing everything. Can't you understand that? Everything?' His hand tightened around the glass until, with a sharp snap, it broke. Bright slivers fell away from his fingers. Whisky darkened with blood dripped to the rug. 'We're Dad's sons. Leigh Merrill's sons. We're entitled to everything there is. We shouldn't have to beg for our own money. We shouldn't have to depend on Elianne. I know what's in her head. Hank will hang around. I guess they'll get married one of these days. That's what she's figuring.'

Mandy made a sharp impatient sound.

'What?' he demanded.

'I told you, and you should listen to me — you don't know what's going on between those two.'

'He'll keep hanging around,' Gordon said firmly. 'That's all I need to know.'

'You're just a babe in arms,' Mandy said. 'You don't know the first thing about what goes on between men and women.'

Gordon shot her a narrow angry look, but he didn't allow himself to be diverted. He said. 'One of these days Elianne's going to figure out an excuse for declaring me incompetent, just wait and see. That's what she wants to do and she'll do it. And Foster Talcott will help her. And then I won't have anything. Not a dime. Nothing. And it'll be the same for you, David. Where will you be if I'm not around to fight your battles for you? Where'll you be if we lose everything?'

David didn't answer.

'That's enough,' Mandy said. She got a towel and wrapped Gordon's hand in it. She said, smiling, 'You worry too much, Gordie. You're scaring David half way to death. You'll see, something'll happen. You're going to get everything you want, and more too.'

'Until now, that's what I thought. But if Hank sticks around, he'll talk Elianne into getting married. That's what he's after. And when that happens, it'll be a whole new ball game as far as David and I are concerned.'

'It hasn't happened yet,' Mandy purred, leaning close to Gordon to plant a deep hot kiss on his mouth.

David backed out of the cottage and gently closed the door behind him.

Carl was sweeping the terrace under the study windows. A newsman was talking about the election returns. Early projections indicated that Jimmy Carter had a substantial lead. But it was only four o'clock. It would be hours before the polls closed across the country. Carl leaned on his broom, considering. He wanted to talk to Elianne. Should he or shouldn't he? Was this a good time? There were all kinds of things on his mind. He didn't know how to sort them out. He had become a fixture at Hannah's Gate. The others so took him for granted that they often didn't notice him. So he heard bits of conversation. He knew, for instance, that when Gordon bought Mandy her car, he'd borrowed all of the money David had saved up in order to pay for it in cash. With his own eyes, Carl had seen Elianne pick up torn bits of paper, and had realized that they were what remained of the notes she had been anxiously looking for before her tests last May. He knew about her near accident at Skyline Drive because he had heard Hank telling Jake about it. Since Keith's death, Carl had not been easy in his mind, just a day before, he had learned that somebody had tried to mug Elianne in a Georgetown night club.

Too many things were happening, that's what Carl told himself. He didn't believe in coincidences. Not when they came one after another. That was why he wanted to talk to Elianne.

Sighing, he put the broom away. He made up an arrangement of dried leaves, and carrying it with him, he went into the house.

Elianne was still in the study, reading.

He asked if he could come in. At her nod, he put the arrangement under the portrait of Big Jack Gowan. He asked if she had a minute.

She closed the book and looked up at him. 'Is something wrong, Carl?'

'No. But there's something on my mind.' He paused. Now he didn't know how to start. Finally, with several false starts, he plunged in, trying to explain that he was at Hannah's Gate under false pretenses, and that he was sorry, and he wanted to set the record straight.

Elianne's eyes widened. She leaned forward. 'Carl, wait a minute. I don't understand. What are you talking about?'

'I know it's confusing,' he said, smiling. 'But the thing is, we're related, Elianne. I knew it when I came here, asking for a job. I didn't mean any harm, I was just curious. And it didn't seem too important. But now . . . now I want you to know. Your grandfather . . . your mother's father, that is . . . Casey Loving.' He paused. When she nodded, he went on, 'Casey Loving had another name, and another family, in New Mexico. Didn't you know he was in New Mexico?'

'I think my mother mentioned it,' Elianne said doubtfully. And then: 'Another family!'

'The Utahs. I guess nobody here ever knew about the Utahs.'

Elianne shook her head.

'Well, I was your grandfather's other son. Your mother's half-brother. Casey Loving called himself Carl Utah when he was in Hobbs. He married my mother under that name. He died when I was about four or so. Later, when I grew up, my mother told me about his Washington family — the Lovings. Your mother, and Hannah's Gate.' Carl smiled at her. 'I never forgot, of course. She wanted to make me feel I had a family some place.'

When he stopped talking there was a silence. She stared at him for a long moment. Then, with a sudden smile, she said, 'You're my half-uncle! It's hard to take it in, but it seems so right. You always seemed so right to me, Carl!'

He said, 'I want you to know that you're not alone, Elianne.' And more softly: 'Do you understand?'

'Not alone,' she repeated. Her hands went to her head and smoothed her hair. She said, 'You should have told me right away. It's so funny, you doing the chores . . . you shouldn't have pretended, Carl.'

'It's what I wanted. What I still want. And there's another thing — could we keep this just between us for the time being?'

'But my brothers . . . Gordon . . . David . . . we ought to tell them.'

'Just for a while.'

'Carl! Why?'

'I don't know exactly. Just an idea I have. Let's not say anything just yet.'

'All right,' she said doubtfully. 'If you're sure . . .'

'I'm sure,' he said, looking relieved. 'We won't tell them. At least not for a while.'

Chapter Fourteen

The room was full of shadows, of rustles and whispers and sighs. Elianne sensed the moving darkness and the sounds, as she drifted on the edge of sleep. Then the rustles and whispers and sighs faded. There was a profound silence, deep and all encompassing. The shadows began to take form. Her mother, Claire. Slender, auburn-haired. Her father, Leigh. Tall, frowning. A small David, listening while a pudgy Gordon spoke softly to him. A headless doll . . . Now a thin faceless figure hovered over her. Her throat tightened on soundless choked back sobs. She was frozen, breathless, but pulses hammering. The hovering figure faded away.

She was suddenly wide awake, staring into the dark with burning eyes, staring at the unmoving shadows. What was there? What had she heard? What had she seen?

The familiar scrape of wistaria gave her comfort. The cold night wind touched her face.

Then she jerked upright to stare across the room. The curtain swayed and swelled on the breeze. The window was wide open. She had closed it before she had gone to bed. She *had* closed it, hadn't she? She could remember struggling with the tight frame. She'd had the same trouble with the latch that she always had. Was that tonight? Or had it been the night before? Now the sense of moving shadows came back to her.

She had been dreaming, of course. Her mother and father. Gordon and David as children. It had been a dream, hadn't it? And the tall figure hovering over her . . . that too must have been part of the dream.

But she continued for a moment to stare at the open window. The more she considered, the more certain she was that she had closed it. But now it was no longer closed.

Eventually she pulled the quilt more tightly around her and turned on her side. After a long while, she fell back asleep.

When she wakened again, the room was full of a grey light. The sky beyond the window was cloudy. A chattering of squirrels came from the nest in the wistaria.

She was relieved that morning had finally come. It had been a bad night, full of dreams that she hardly remembered now, even though they had left her feeling tired and troubled.

She told herself to forget the night. She rose, ready to start the day.

Today she braided her long hair, wrapping it into a thick coil on the top of her head. She put on black trousers, a white shirt, and over it a black and white sleeveless sweater. As she turned to leave the room, something about her desk caught her eye. Something peculiar. An empty space at the far corner. Suddenly she realized that that was where she kept her mother's copy of *Sonnets from the Portuguese*, the love poems Ollie had given her mother, and then Elianne after her mother's death.

She quickly went to the desk, looked at the letters in the centre, the glass of pencils. It was no use. The book wasn't there. She instantly remembered the lost notes that she had later found under the rose bushes on the terrace. She wondered whether one day she would find the remnants of the love poems too. With a sigh, she went to the door then stopped. She turned back to look at the window. It was still open, the curtains billowing. The open window . . . the missing book . . . the dreams of moving shadows . . . A shiver rippled through her.

She quickly closed the door behind her, and hurried downstairs. On the table in the foyer was a large vase of brilliant yellow chrysan-

251

themums. Carl had been in early as always. How strange that all this time she had had a half-uncle and hadn't known it. Secrets . . . Hannah's Gate was full of them. She had always felt that. Sensed the secrets, heard the angry whispers. And now there was one more: Carl. She wondered why he didn't want anyone except her to know about their relationship yet. She didn't know why, but she trusted him. That's why she had agreed to say nothing. She would wait, as she'd promised to. Perhaps soon he'd change his mind.

Irene had set the table as always. There was coffee on a hot plate. Fruit juice in a jug. Bowls of dry cereal. A creamer with milk, and a bowl of sugar, both china brought back from London long ago by her mother.

David was there, reading the paper. He nodded at her, and moments after she sat down, rose, saying he was going to be late for school if he didn't get a move on. She heard him climb the stairs. After a moment he returned. He was whistling when he went out.

Hank and Jake were nearly finished eating. 'Sleep well?' Hank asked.

She nodded, avoiding his eyes. Memories of the dream still clung to her. The hovering figure . . . the drapes billowing at the open window . . . She said nothing about the missing book, nor her dream.

Jake spoke of going downtown for a few hours, and asked if she wanted to go with him.

She told him she had things to do and had better stay at home.

He said he'd be around for a while, in case she changed her mind, and then emptied his coffee cup and went to the new wing.

She drank some juice, had cereal with sugar and milk, and a cup of coffee. Hank stayed with her until she had finished. They parted in the foyer. He was going to see Charlie Carroll, and planned to spend the rest of the day at the detective agency. She went upstairs to her room.

She didn't realize at first that anything was wrong. Irene had asked if she had any old clothes to donate to her church, so Elianne was going through her closet, considering what she could still use, what she would no longer wear.

Suddenly the hanging garments began to sway, to ripple, to shrink and expand as she stared at them.

She stepped back, a pulse thudding in her throat. She was gripped with cold, but her fingers and toes were burning.

She sat down at her desk, and stared at a letter. The words became small black ants racing wildly on the grainy sand of the white page. She whimpered aloud without hearing the sound of it on her lips.

From outside there were faint rattles and scrapes as Carl worked below the window. To her, those everyday noises were as loud as thunder. Her ears felt assaulted by great roaring vibrations.

The room seemed to be filled with a noxious odour. An emanation of rot, decay. What stank so? Why did the noise hurt? She swung her head from side to side. What was happening? The walls were shining with a brilliance that stung her eyes so that they filled with tears. The blue curtains writhed at the window. The sunlight swelled and faded, brightened and dimmed.

'Oh, God,' she whispered. 'Oh, God, no, no . . . please, no. Don't let it happen. Don't let it come back again.' And even as she spoke the words, she saw the flashing of splintered glass, and the small falling body of the tiny girl. She saw the limp body hit the ground, the myriad wounds leaking red. And the blood became small red worms.

She leaped from the chair. It fell over with a crash. She backed into the corner, twisting, turning, her hands covering her eyes, crouching low to escape the vision. Finally, unable to escape, she curled into a ball, knees to her face, arms hugging her body.

Writhing, twisting, lashed by pain, icy cold and burning heat. Bones melting. Flesh freezing. Lucid by moments. 'Oh, please, oh, no. Not a flashback. Not after all this time. Oh, please . . . please . . . how can it happen?' And then, the wild gibberish: 'Ella Em . . . Ella Em.'

Ella Em was screaming. The red worms crawled on her body. In her eyes. Her ears. Her nose. Her mouth. She rose to her feet, and ran into the hallway, screams trailing her.

Irene was at the foot of the stairs. She held out her arms. 'Elianne! What's wrong? What's happened?'

But Elianne spun away, raced down the hall and into the kitchen. She flung the door open and dashed outside. Hoarse now, she shouted wordlessly, her face tilted towards the sky.

Carl dropped his tools, came running. 'What is it, Elianne! Stop! Wait!'

But she was running still. She tore at her clothes, arms thrashing. She pulled at her braids until they came down, fell unbounded on her shoulders. Then she tore at her flowing hair. And the wordless shouts went on and on.

Jake was in the new wing. He heard her. He ran out. Suddenly he was in her path. She tried to dodge around him, but he swept her into his arms. He held her tight against his body. 'Wait, Elianne. Wait now. It's me. It's Jake! You know me, Elianne.' His voice was soft, crooning. He held her tightly, pressing her face into his shoulder so that her screams were muted now. He held her tightly, pressing her arms between them, so that they were trapped and still. Softly and slowly he said, 'You're all right. It'll be over soon. Nothing's happening to you. Nothing, Elianne. It'll be over soon.' As he spoke, he drew her with him. 'Now you're better. See? You can walk, Elianne. You're okay. It'll be over soon.' He half-carried, half-walked her, feet dragging, body sagging within his grasp.

'A doctor?' Irene asked.

Carl stood frowning, silent.

Jake shook his head. 'No, no. She's going to be okay. I know what to do.' He held Elianne close. 'I know what to do, don't I?'

He got her into his room in the new wing. He put her into a big chair near the window, and threw it open so that the cold air blew on her face. He sat beside her, holding both her hands. 'Now we're going to be quiet. We're going to keep our eyes closed, and rest, and breathe slowly. And after a while we're going to sleep a little. And pretty soon it'll be all over. It'll be gone. I promise you, Elianne. It'll be gone.'

Gradually her cries grew further and further

apart until she sank into silence. Her eyes finally closed. Her breath slowed. She sagged against the chair back, her body limp, no longer twitching. Her clutching fingers relaxed within his grasp.

For a while, he was perfectly still, watching her. His mind was blank. He refused to allow himself to think. When he was certain that she had fallen into a normal sleep, he put her hands in her lap. Then he waited again. She didn't move or respond.

He got up and went to the closet to look in his backpack. He took out his stash. The pouch and papers were as he had left them. He examined the pills. Maybe there were fewer. Maybe there weren't. He should have counted them at some time or other, then he'd know for certain. But he hadn't bothered. He should have got rid of them a long time ago. He hadn't done that either.

He put the pouch and papers into the backpack. But he took the pills into the bathroom and flushed them away. Too late, but done now.

He went to look at Elianne. She was still sleeping. He sat down to wait. He would have to tell her when she woke up. But before he did, he'd better figure it out himself. Who? How? He went over in his mind what he knew. When had he last looked at the stuff in the cupboard? Who could have been into it? And what had happened this morning? First, Carl had been in for breakfast when Jake himself went down. Hank and David came in later, talking about the election that Carter had just won.

Elianne's cereal bowl had been sitting on the table . . .

In late afternoon Elianne awakened. She was pale, her eyes ringed with dark shadows. 'It was terrible,' she said to Jake. 'I couldn't believe it was really happening.'

'I know. I could see that it was. A really bad trip. Worse than you ever had.'

'I was sure it wouldn't happen, Jake. Not after all this time. I don't see why it did, what triggered it. I've been fine. I'd almost forgotten that I'd ever done acid.' She looked into his face. 'Truly, Jake. Truly. I haven't touched the stuff, not since . . . since I left Taos. I swear I haven't. So how could I have had a flashback now?'

He fingered his chin as if wishing the beard he had shaven off were still there. Finally he said, 'You didn't have a flashback, Elianne.'

'But I must have, Jake. What else could it have been?'

He didn't answered her. This was hard, harder than he'd thought it would be. It was

258

his fault. He hated to admit it to her.

She stared at him for a long time. Then: 'Tell me, Jake.'

'You didn't drop acid yourself?'

'Jake! No! How could I?'

'Okay.' He paused to take a deep breath. Then: 'So somebody gave it to you.'

'But that's impossible,' she protested. 'There isn't any around. And where would somebody get it?'

'There's some around, Elianne. Or rather, there was.'

'Oh, Jake. You had some, didn't you?'

He nodded. 'I haven't been using. Not for a long time. But I had it.' He added quickly, 'I don't have it any more. I threw it down the toilet a while ago.'

'I asked you not to bring anything into the house, Jake. Don't you remember? I asked you.'

'I know. I'm sorry. But here's the important thing: somebody fed it to you, Elianne.'

'But why? Who?'

'I've been asking myself the same question.'

She shivered violently. 'I'm scared.'

'Don't be. It won't happen again. The stuff's gone. It's going to be okay.'

Later, when she was alone, she kept remembering how Jake's face had looked when he told her what he thought had happened. He seemed so sure of what he was saying. He seemed so honest. But she found herself doubting him. He was the only one who knew about LSD. He'd used it, and often, years before. He admitted that he'd brought it with him, had it in the house. He'd realized immediately what was happening to her.

He'd said she'd probably taken it at breakfast that morning. Hank had been at the table. David too. Carl was gone before she came in, but he'd been there earlier. She didn't know if Gordon had come up to the house for breakfast while Mandy was sleeping, as he occasionally did. Any one of them could have crumbled a pill into her cereal. Once she'd added sugar and milk, she'd never have tasted it. But, as far as she knew for certain, only Jake would have known that. Only Jake. But why would he have done it, then told her? Why? He was changed now. Could he possibly want her to be Ella Em again?

Jake was pretty sure what had happened to Elianne. But only pretty sure. That's why he hadn't told her straight out what he was thinking. He was pretty sure, but he didn't have any proof. David. That's who he had settled on. He dismissed Hank. He was in love with Elianne. Besides, he wouldn't have known how to handle LSD, or where to find it. He considered Gordon, but dismissed him too. Gordon was too wrapped up in Mandy to think about anything else, and Jake didn't see him as a risk-taker anyhow. Carl? No. True, there was something peculiar about Carl, but if you watched how he looked at Elianne, you'd know he'd never hurt her. So Jake settled on David. Silent David, who'd had ample opportunity to go into Jake's room. David whom Jake had more than once observed climbing in the wistaria on the back wall of the house. Jake settled on David, but he didn't know what he ought to do about it.

He decided he'd better keep his own counsel for a little while. He'd better think on it. And he'd better stick close to the house and watch David until he knew what to do.

The mingled laughter from the games room drew Jake. Gordon and Mandy were there. So was David.

Jake ambled down the hall.

The room was bright, the windows black with night sky.

Gordon was bending over the pool table, cue in hand, squinting at the triangle of coloured balls.

Mandy was saying, 'I'll bet you anything you say . . .' Her glance slid sideways to where Jake leaned against the wall, watching.

He chuckled, and fingered his bare chin. He was almost accustomed to being clean shaven, but every once in a while he missed the beard. This was one of those times. He felt exposed. Maybe because of what he was thinking.

Neither Gordon nor David paid any attention to him. But Mandy said, 'Hi, what're you up to?'

'Just hanging around.'

Gordon darted a look at him, puckered his lips in a silent whistle. 'Mandy, you'd better watch this. Since you're betting.'

But she raised the volume on the transistor, snapped her fingers and tapped her toe to the loud music. 'Come on, Jake. Let's give it a whirl.' When he hesitated, she cried, 'Come on. Don't tell me you don't know how to dance all of a sudden.' She didn't wait for him to move. She came and caught him in her arms, thrusting her body against his. Close. Warm. Inviting.

For a few steps he followed her lead, but then he took over. Stepping back. Separating. Only their fingertips touched. Their rolling thrusting hips pounded out the rhythm of the drums. Mandy's red curls bounced. Her breasts bounced.

David slouched in an easy chair, throwing a ping pong ball from his right hand to his left, his left to his right. He watched expressionlessly.

Gordon shot one quick look after another at the dancing couple. Their eyes were locked. Their smiling lips glistened. Their hips rolled. A thick sour nausea climbed into Gordon's throat. He couldn't breathe. Suddenly he threw down his cue. He yelled, 'Okay, Mandy. That's enough!' And to Jake: 'What do you think you're doing?'

'What's wrong with you?' Jake demanded. But he was smiling.

'Boys,' Mandy said. 'Now, boys.' Laughing, she tossed her curls. 'What's a dance or two, Gordie?' She linked her arm through his. 'Come on, Gordie. What's the fuss about? All I want is a little fun!'

He glared at Jake, but allowed Mandy to lead him from the room.

As they left to return to the cottage, Mandy clinging to Gordon, they passed Elianne.

She went on into the games room. Jake was leaning against the pool table, chalking a cue. She asked what the yelling had been about. Jake shrugged, but David told her what had happened.

'I suppose I shouldn't tease Gordon,' Jake said. 'But sometimes I can't help it.' Grinning he added, 'Mandy can't help teasing him either.'

David punched a button on the jukebox. The room vibrated to the loud music: *Pistol Packin' Mama*.

Elianne felt like a child again. Lost, frightened, unloved. It was her father's favourite song. David was staring at her with blank eyes. Soon he would play *The White Cliffs of Dover*. Another of her father's favourite songs.

She put her hands over her ears, and backed slowly from the room.

Late one night, at the end of the week, David sat close by the woodpile on the terrace behind the house. He could see the whole of the property from there. The pool with its dark blue tarpaulin covering, and the cottage, and the brick wall that faced Afton Place. He could also see, by looking out of the corner of his eye, an angle of the new wing.

Jake was at the window of his room.

David could feel his eyes. Speculative, watchful. Deep seeing. His silhouette was clear and sharp, but unfamiliar still. To David, the shaven chin and short hair made him seem a stranger. He *was* a stranger, David told himself. He didn't belong in Hannah's Gate.

Jake had been ever present all week. David had become more and more aware of him. It had been possible to escape him only by hiding inside his own room, David told himself. Go anywhere else in the house — the study, the kitchen, the dining room, or games room — and Jake would be there too. Go outside to the front, hang around in the driveway, walk through the yard, and pretty soon Jake would turn up.

He was so obvious about it that it would have made David laugh. Except that it wasn't funny. Jake had something on his mind. David was beginning to feel fairly sure that he knew what it was.

Now, as David was thinking about it, Jake disappeared from the window. Within moments he came out of the house, stopped as if seeing David for the first time, as if he hadn't been watching him from the window. Then he walked over to sit down beside him.

Jake leaned back against the woodpile and folded his arms. 'Quiet time?'

David nodded, didn't speak.

'Not that it's ever noisy time with you.'

David continued the blank-eyed look.

'You never say much,' Jake went on.

'I don't have much to say,' David said at last.

Jake didn't know if he was going about it the right way. He wasn't sure of what he was doing. Maybe he was wrong. Still, he had to take that chance. Right now it seemed that going straight to the point was the only way.

He said, 'Oh, I'll bet you've got plenty to say, if only you wanted to.'

'Me?' David suddenly laughed.

'You,' Jake said. He made up his mind in that instant. Right or wrong, he would have to take the chance. The only way to stop David from whatever he was trying to do to Elianne was to warn him off. To let him know he was discovered. He was found out. That was how Jake could keep Elianne safe. 'Listen, David, I know you went into my room, and got into my stuff. I know about what you've been trying to do to Elianne.' His voice was calm, conversational, his eyes steady on David's face. They glowed as they had once done when he had said, 'Love is Divine. Believe in Love and you believe in the Divine.'

David saw the light in his eyes. He heard the words. It took moments for the meaning to sink in. Finally, in spite of the calm voice and unthreatening expression, the meaning penetrated.

David didn't stop to think, to consider. With understanding came movement, all of a piece, knit together as one. He reached behind him and pulled a heavy piece of cut wood from the pile. He brought it forward in a swift swinging motion, and clubbed Jake across the forehead.

Jake groaned and instantly fell forward.

David scrambled to his feet. He caught Jake under the arms and dragged him down the steps, across the lower terrace to the concrete apron. He rolled Jake's body across it to the edge of the pool. He let Jake rest until he had lifted up the tarpaulin. Then, with a quick heave, he shoved Jake into the icy water, and dropped the cover back into place.

Jake was gone.

David raised his arms over his head, and stretched high and wide.

After a while, he went back to the terrace and got the club he had used. Half an hour later, he dropped it into the canal near Fletcher's Landing. Before he left, he took the book of Elizabeth Barrett Browning's love poems, ripped it to pieces, and ground them underfoot in the mud of the towpath.

Chapter Fifteen

On Monday morning, Elianne came into the dining room at breakfast time. Hank was there, just finishing his coffee. David was on her heels. He slid into his chair without speaking.

She heard Carl's deep rumbling voice in the hallway and Irene's soft murmur.

It crossed Elianne's mind that she ought to tell everyone about Carl. Gordon and David had the right to know. She brushed the thought away. Not now. At the moment there was something else. Aloud she asked, 'Has anybody seen Jake yet this morning?'

'He hasn't been in,' Hank said. He wondered why Elianne had that worried look. Jake could take care of himself. Of that, Hank was certain. Besides, he didn't give a damn about Jake.

Plainly Elianne did. She let the guy stay on and on. For no reason. And ever since she had had that weird attack, he'd noticed that

Jake seemed to be ever present. Hank had been at the detective agency when it happened, but he'd heard from Irene how Jake had taken care of her, and brought her out of it. When Hank asked Elianne what had happened, and said she should see a doctor, she had refused to talk about it, closing him out the way she always did nowadays. That had hurt, but it had made him angry too. He couldn't accept her disinterest in him. He supposed he ought to give up, but he loved her and wasn't going to let her go.

She was saying, 'Did either of you see him yesterday?'

David shook his head.

'I don't think so,' Hank told her. He rose. 'I'm going to the agency. Call me, if you want me.'

'It's odd,' she said. 'I don't think he was around yesterday. But I'm not sure.'

'You know Jake,' Hank said. 'He comes and goes.' Hank checked his watch. Charlie was a lot better, but he still wasn't ready to return to work. Hank hoped he'd be able to take over soon. Hank didn't like going away from Hannah's Gate every day. He had the feeling that things were happening that he didn't know about. It bothered him. But he didn't know what to do. If only there was somebody he could trust. But who? He was suspicious of Jake, had been ever since he first saw him. He didn't know anything about Carl Utah, a guy Gordon said he'd picked up in a bar. Gordon himself? David? Mandy? He knew those three all right. But where did that get him? Ever since Hallowe'en night, when somebody had grabbed Elianne in the night club corridor, Hank had become certain that she was in some sort of danger. That's why he always told her where he'd be, said she should call him if she wanted him. He continuously examined the evidence in his mind. First there'd been the destroyed research notes. Then there came the near-miss at Skyline Drive. Keith had died immediately after. Much later there'd been the attack in the night club. Within days she'd had the screaming fit that Jake had brought her out of. He knew it was hopeless to try to talk to her about it. So he didn't. But he worried all the same. Now he rose. At the door, he turned back to say, 'Remember, Elianne. If you need me, just give me a call.'

She nodded absently. After he had gone, she said, 'I don't understand it. I have the feeling Jake hasn't been around for several days.'

David looked up from his scrambled eggs. 'He'll turn up.'

She didn't answer. She had a spoonful of

cereal, half a cup of coffee. But at last she pushed the food aside. She couldn't eat. Suppose something had happened again. Suppose, in a little while, she was stricken once more with those awful images, and couldn't breathe, and couldn't think. Jake wasn't here. Who would help her? Who would know how to? Where could Jake be? Would he have gone away without saying a word to her? Maybe, once, he would have. But not any more. He had changed. She kept trying to remember when she had last seen him. Not yesterday. She was becoming certain of that. The day before? She wasn't sure.

She tried to recall when she had last noticed a light in his window during the evening. From her own room, she could see only a bit of the new wing. But the light from his window usually made a rectangle on the terrace beneath it when he had his lamp on. When had she last noticed that rectangle of light? Had it been two nights ago? Three?

She got up, went out to the porch. The air was cold, damp. Her breath made a white cloud before her face. Jake's van was where he usually parked it. Inside again, shivering a little, she decided to check out his room. She was beginning to think she'd last seen him a few evenings ago in the games room. Gordon had been jealous, yelling at Jake and Mandy.

271

As she walked down the corridor of the new wing, she passed by the group of photographs her father had hung there years before. She glanced at them, but didn't pause to look at them closely. She already knew that each was of David and Gordon. She was present in only one, and in that, she was off to the side. The pictures had perfectly captured the way it had been for her. She was absent from the group or in the one where she was present, she stood alone, separate, while her father, tall, smiling faintly, held David in his arms, and Gordon stood pressed close to him, round face bright with adoration. That was how it had been. She stood alone, the space between her father and brothers and herself an uncrossable chasm. Her mother was absent entirely, perhaps holding the camera. Elianne wasn't sure. She didn't remember when these various pictures had been taken. Whatever the real reason for her mother's absence, it was symbolic. Because that was how it had been. Her father and brothers . . . Her mother and herself . . . The two groups divided. Not one family. A divided family. It was so sad. And sadder still that it continued, although it was far less open than when she had been a child.

Most of the time Gordon and David were courteous and amenable, even though they did as they pleased. But sometimes Gordon would flare up in a temper, then offer a smiling apology. David was wrapped in perpetual silence. Yet in both of them she sensed hostility. She was beginning to feel that they, along with everyone else at Hannah's Gate, Jake, Hank, Carl, Mandy, were all like the painted figures on the walls of the Armagosa Opera House at Death Valley Junction. Their faces and bodies appeared to be real, their poses and movements and clothes too. But in reality they were one-dimensional works of oil and dye on board, masks behind which the truth hid. Then who could she turn to? Who could she trust?

In front of Jake's room, she paused and listened. She hoped to hear him moving around inside: humming, or coughing, or flipping through the pages of a book. But there was no sound from within. No sound at all in the new wing. A thick and empty silence had descended on the house.

She knocked lightly, waited. She knocked again, louder this time. Finally she pushed the door open. The air was heavy, warm, with a tinge of familiar sweetness. She frowned. Jake had smoked pot in here at some time or other. The odour of it had clung to the curtains and rug. He'd promised he wouldn't have drugs in Hannah's Gate, but he had. Pot. Acid. What else? He could have had almost anything. But he'd said he'd got rid of it. He'd told her that. She shivered. He'd told her a lot of things.

Slowly, unwillingly, she went to the dresser. It took her only moments to check the few drawers. He had come with little, and still owned little. His underclothes and shirts were neatly arranged. There were a couple of pairs of socks. His beads were still there, the shell necklaces, the skull carved from bone. He hadn't worn them since he'd shaven off his beard. In the cupboard there was the black denim jacket he used to wear, two pairs of jeans, a pair of boots. Everything he owned was still here. She saw his backpack on the top shelf and took it down. Inside she found a couple of worn paperbacks, an edition of the Bible that was falling apart. A roll of tissue paper. She smoothed it out. There was nothing inside. Nothing. But she was able to guess what it had once held, even though he'd told her the truth, she realized now, when he said he'd got rid of the drugs. A small pouch with a few crumbs of marijuana. A packet of cigarette papers.

Plainly, he hadn't gone. She couldn't imagine him leaving for good and abandoning the little he owned behind. It was all that he had except for what he was wearing. He no longer wore the old stuff. He had shaved his beard and cut his hair. Still, she didn't see him leaving these things behind. And certainly not the Bible. No, it was impossible. Jake wasn't gone.

Yet the room felt abandoned. The bed was made, the spread smooth and unwrinkled. The curtains were drawn against the grey light of day. The ash tray was clean. The place was lifeless. It was as if no one had breathed there, slept there, dreamed there, for a very long time.

Bewildered, more uneasy than ever, she backed slowly from the room, telling herself that since his belongings were here and his van was in the driveway, he was here too. Or, if he wasn't then he'd be returning soon.

She waited through the rest of the day, attending to her chores, doing her cheque book and accounts, but all the time she listened for the sound of his voice. She awaited the sound of his footsteps. She was sure he hadn't gone away for good. But there was a vague core of concern in her. Where was he? Why didn't he turn up?

While she was going over her cheque book, reconciling the balance, she noticed something wrong with one of the cheques. It was for two hundred and fifty-seven dollars, made out to Saks Wisconsin Avenue. She'd often shopped there, but hadn't been there in several months. For a moment, she stared at it, confused. Perhaps she just didn't remember the purchase. But when she examined the register, she saw that there was no entry for that cheque number. She was nowhere near it, in fact. She looked more carefully, and found that one had been taken from the back of the cheque book. She certainly hadn't done that. Her heart sank. She knew what must have happened. The cheque book was always here, in the top drawer of the desk. Someone had taken a cheque out, and forged her signature.

Could it have been Jake? Had he needed money to leave? But no. It was impossible. He was still here.

Besides she knew who it was, who it had to be: Gordon. Gordon, who was always short of money, and who had proven a dozen times that he had no scruples. The car he'd bought for Mandy stood outside in the driveway. It was proof, if nothing else was, that he didn't care what he did. He'd paid for it in cash, using every cent he could get his hands on, and taking all of David's money too. He had admitted that only when she challenged him about it. She had tried to stop it, but had been too late. The purchase had been finalized, the money paid. Mandy owned the car outright. That was that. Elianne hadn't even consulted Foster Talcott about it. But now there was this. Would Gordon have forged her signature? It seemed possible. She decided she would have to find out.

But, in the meantime, what had happened to Jake?

Later she heard Hank return. She thought of talking it over with him, but decided against it. It wasn't fair to use him, to depend on him. Not any more. She supposed he wouldn't mind. He might even welcome her confiding in him. There were moments, still, when she longed for him. But there had been a time when she longed for Jake. She didn't know what love was, what her feelings meant. It was over between her and Hank, and she had to keep it that way. He had spoiled their love when he asked her to marry him. With that thought came a wave of cold panic. The same cold panic she had felt when he first spoke of marriage. In response, she had broken off their affair. So she couldn't talk to Hank.

She would have to deal with Gordon on her own. She slipped on a heavy jacket, thinking that she didn't want to accuse Gordon of stealing one of her cheques, forging her signature. If only she could find some other way of learning what had happened. If he was the person responsible. Did the store have a record of what had been bought, who had bought it? It seemed unlikely since a cheque was handled as if it were cash. Still, it was possible. But before she went any further, she had to make sure she hadn't bought anything for two hundred and fifty-seven dollars, and then forgotten about it. She returned to the study and found the last statement she had received from Saks. Nothing. But then she realized that a cheque wouldn't have shown up on her charge account. She called the Saks Credit Department. After explaining the problem several times, she spoke to someone who, with the cheque number, and the sales check number written on that, was able to trace the purchase. It was from the Ladies Leather Goods section: a pouch bag of burgundy-coloured suede. Elianne instantly remembered Mandy talking about her new pouch bag. Elianne didn't see how Mandy could have taken one of her cheques, but Gordon could have. And Gordon could have forged her signature. He and Mandy always shopped together. It was Mandy's favourite pastime.

Sighing, Elianne started for the cottage again. She would have to talk to Gordon. Much as she hated to, she would have to. Forgery was criminal. He couldn't be allowed to get away with it. Not even this one time. She would have to put the fear of God in him, and get Foster Talcott to do the same.

But she didn't get to the cottage. Carl came hurrying from the house to tell her that there was a phone call for her. It turned out to be Stacy Grayson.

Elianne decided that her talk with Gordon and Mandy could wait a few minutes. It had been some time since she had spoken to Stacy. She didn't want to seem unfriendly or rude.

She went back to the study. Stacy greeted her, then told her that Anna Taylor, her grandmother, wasn't well. She'd expressed the desire to see Elianne.

'She doesn't have much interest in anything or anybody any more,' Stacy said. 'So if you wouldn't mind . . . We'd really appreciate it . . .' And she added, 'Grandma's not always quite there, you know. She gets confused.'

'When is a good time for me to come?' Elianne asked.

'This evening? Right after dinner? We don't know how long . . .' Stacy paused, then added quickly, 'Oh, I almost forgot, Grandma's at Mother's house now.'

Elianne arrived at the Grayson house at seven-thirty. As she rang the doorbell she remembered the first time she had been there. The garden party that had ended so badly. Garet Morley falling, as blood spread on his jacket . . . the sound of sirens . . . the flash camera's sudden glare . . .

Inside, she found Stacy and Garet, and Stacy's mother too. Anna Taylor lay on a sofa in the living room, propped on pillows. She raised her head to smile at Elianne. 'Why, my dear,' she said in a whisper. 'What a pretty girl you are! And how much you resemble your mother Claire.'

For a moment, Elianne saw within the framework of the withered flesh a hint of a younger woman, within the shrunken form a bare outline of the big-bosomed, curved and corseted body she once had. Then her vision cleared. She saw Anna Taylor as she was now: aged and ill, a wheel chair beside the sofa. Instantly she thought of Keith. Instantly she wondered again what had happened to him, and how he had died. Swiftly she shifted her glance away from the wheel chair.

Anna Taylor was saying, 'It's been so long since I've seen you. Why, surely, it's not since that awful night here. Do you remember it? When Garet was attacked by those terrible men!'

'Now, Grandma,' Stacy interrupted, 'don't think of that. Let's remember all the good things.' She patted her rounded belly as a reminder. She was carrying a great-grandchild for her grandmother to look forward to. That was a good thing, wasn't it?

The older woman smiled obediently, but her attention remained on Elianne. 'It was such a bad thing,' she said. 'And afterwards you became a recluse, didn't you? Oh, Elianne, that was wrong of you. Forgive me for saying so but when the worst happens, you mustn't withdraw. Think of your Grandmother Dora.' Anna's voice trailed away with the name. Her eyes slowly closed. Her small wrinkled hands, flashing the rings that were loose on her fingers, fluttered like dried leaves and then were still on the shawl that covered her.

After a moment or two, Elianne gathered herself to rise.

But at her first faint movement, Anna opened her eyes, saying, 'Why, Claire! How good of you to come to see me. And how you do resemble your dear mother. Oh, I miss her. It's terrible to be the last one left, the only one left. We did have such good conversations.'

'You were good friends,' Elianne said softly.

'We were. Although Dora did make it difficult. She was so hurt by what happened. Big Jack was her idol, and rightly so. He was a loving father to her. But he was a scamp, of course. So many men are. Still, scamp or no, it wasn't true about the bribery. It certainly wasn't. Yet it hurt Dora to see him die a broken old man. And her Casey . . . he was a scamp too, I suppose, although I never knew it for certain.' Anna stopped. 'Casey . . . I'm sorry, Claire. I oughtn't to have said that. Forgive an old lady. I simply forgot for a moment that Casey was your father, Claire.'

Elianne thought of Carl Utah, Casey Loving's son. Yes, Anna Taylor was right. Her grandfather had certainly been what the older woman called a scamp. But what had happened to him? Why had he had a second family in New Mexico?

Stacy, exasperated, said loudly, 'Grandma, this is Elianne Merrill. Not Claire. Claire's her mother. You're getting all mixed up.'

There was a pause. Anna studied Elianne, then smiled. 'Oh, yes, I know,' she said quietly. And to Stacy: 'You needn't raise your voice. I hear perfectly well.' She turned back to Elianne. 'It's been so long. Your Grandmother Dora did the same as you. She withdrew. When they became poor, she hid in Hannah's Gate. As if it mattered to me, to anyone else. It only mattered to her. Your mother now — Claire, I mean — she was a fighter. I remember so well how it was. Your father was overseas during the war, in a prison camp, and listed as missing in action. Claire never gave up. Never. That's what Dora told me. Sometimes, when I insisted, I got Dora to come here, spend a little time with me. It was good for her to get away from Hannah's Gate. I knew it then, I know it now, she knew it too, Elianne — there were secrets in Hannah's Gate, she would tell me. Whispering. Bad things. She feared it was like a disease, contagious, hereditary. Something awful that lurked there and came out, time after time, in each generation . . . Poor Dora . . .' Once again Anna's voice drifted off. Her eyes closed slowly. Her hands fluttered on her shawl and were still.

Elianne got up. She whispered, 'I'll come back again soon.'

Anna Taylor's head moved in a nod.

Elianne pressed a kiss on her wrinkled cheek, and hurried to the door.

Stacy followed her. 'I'm sorry, Elianne. You never know with Grandma, as I told you. All that nonsense about secrets, and Hannah's Gate, and diseases. You just can't tell what she's going to come up with.'

Elianne left quickly, anxious to leave behind her Anna Taylor's troubling words. But of course they went with her.

Whispering. Bad things. A contagious disease at Hannah's Gate. Anna Taylor's soft voice spoke in Elianne's mind as she parked in the driveway. She got out of the car. A cold wind tugged at her hair as she passed the tall magnolia and went into the house.

A note on the foyer table told her that Hank had gone back to Charlie Carroll's office for an hour or so. After she read it, Elianne put it down next to the poinsettia Carl had left there.

Secrets. Anna Taylor was right, Elianne knew. Carl was one of them. Casey Loving's son, born of a marriage no one here had known about. And there were others. She had long sensed the current of hidden events, and wondered at them. She had heard angry whispers in the night when she was a child. Her Grandmother Dora had heard them too. Old secrets. And new ones.

Elianne stood still, listening. There was silence. But within the silence there were the small sighings and creakings of an ageing house. She shook her head. Never mind. She had something she must do. Much as she didn't want to, she would have to. She went into the study, found the cheque with her forged signature and went out through the back door.

She had to talk to Gordon. She would tell him that she wouldn't allow him to forge her name. She would inform him that she was going to return the cheque to the bank, and tell them what he had done. This time, but this time only, she wouldn't press charges. But the bank would know it would have to be on the lookout, and would be certain to examine carefully any cheques of hers that came in.

She found, when she went outside, that the

air felt strange. It was still cold, but now seemed tinged with a faint warmth. In the distance lightning flickered and danced through the darkness. The tree limbs swayed restlessly, scraping each other.

Lights glowed in the cottage, but no one answered when she knocked. She waited for a little while, then gave up, and started back to the house.

As she walked along the concrete apron beside the pool, she heard a car pull into the driveway. Headlights flashed briefly. Maybe it was Hank coming home. Or maybe Jake had arrived by taxi. The wind was blowing harder now. It was warmer too. More lightning flashed in the west. Thunder rumbled. The pool cover rose up, billowing like a sail. When it collapsed it hit the water with a sharp slapping sound. The logs Carl had put in it to prevent freeze damage thudded against the tiles. A shower of dry leaves blew against her. The wind whipped her hair across her face. She hurried around the corner of the pool towards the steps. The wind gusted, catching the cheque in her hand. It was torn from her fingers, and fell on to the pool cover only inches from the edge.

She cried out, and bent to snatch it back before it sailed beyond reach. By stretching forward, she just managed to catch it. Then, off balance, she teetered at the rim of the pool. For what seemed to her long moments, she rocked back and forth, while the wind thrust her forward, and she fought to throw herself backward to safety.

At last she pitched herself away by thrusting down on the tarpaulin. There was an awful instant when it gave way, the log beneath strangely soft. Then she went sprawling, fingers still clenched around the cheque.

She waited, caught her breath, and got to her feet. The wind was still blowing hard. The tarpaulin billowed and flapped, rising and falling. She stared at the long rounded forms of the logs outlined when the cover lay briefly on the surface of the water. She stared at them, counting. One. Two. Three. Four. Five. Yes, there were five. But she could almost hear Carl telling her that he would put in three or four logs to keep the water from freezing over the winter, expanding, and cracking the pool tiles. She remembered wondering how he had known that. Five logs. Not two or three. Five.

She told herself that she was allowing her imagination to run away with her. She was permitting Anna Taylor's words to infect her. She told herself to stop. Just stop. But so much had happened. She thought of Keith, and how he died. She remembered her wild search for her research notes, and at the same time asked herself what had happened to her mother's book of poems. She saw in her mind the tumbling boulder that tore across the path where she had walked only moments before. She shuddered, once again feeling the hands of the masked devil who had grabbed her in the Georgetown night club. She saw again the black print turn into angry ants on the white page, and heard herself screaming in the bad acid trip. And she hadn't taken LSD, at least not knowingly. Now Jake was gone.

She wanted to turn away, to go into the house. A car had come in. Probably it was Hank. She wanted to talk to him. She wanted to tell him everything she feared. She wanted more than anything to go away from the place near the pool as quickly as she could.

But she remained there, the wind blowing her hair, pulling at her skirt, thunder vibrating from the sky. And finally she bent down. She removed the three cinder blocks that Carl had placed at the corner to secure the cover. She lifted them off and put them aside one by one. The wind immediately peeled the tarpaulin up and back, raised it up like a dark blue sail, and then grabbed it and flung it over.

The water rippled, reflections of light dancing along its moving surface. But amid the dancing reflections there was a still place, a dark one. It was log-shaped, but not a log. The body lay on the moving surface, drifting gently. A body, swollen within its wet clothing. A body. A man's body. Jake's.

Elianne covered her face with her hands and screamed.

Chapter Sixteen

Honey Locust Lane was quiet now. The ambulance and police cars were gone, along with the mobile crime unit. The small crowd of curious onlookers had wandered away.

Two men came out of Hannah's Gate and climbed into a dark sedan. They were the last to depart, detectives from the Homicide Squad.

One was tall and thin. He had close-cropped black curly hair, and wore a thick black moustache. His eyes were a faded blue. He had noticeably large ears, which stuck out from his head. They made him seem younger than thirty-seven. His name was William Eagan, but most people called him Bill, although his mother still called him Junior.

He said to his partner, 'I've never been here before but I know this house. My Dad used to talk about it, back when I was a kid after World War II. Some funny things happened here. A couple of girls were killed by a spy.

289

But it looks bigger than it used to. The walls weren't here then. And there's a new wing. A lot of changes.'

His partner said, 'One thing's the same. Somebody's been killed again.'

Bill Eagan sighed. 'It looks like it. We'll have to wait for the medical examiner's report, but I'm pretty sure. We'll stop by tomorrow and talk to everybody again.'

They drove away, leaving the street empty and silent.

Inside Hannah's Gate, Elianne stared at Hank, whispering, 'What are we going to do?'

'We'll wait and see what happens.'

She shuddered, held tightly to her coffee mug with both hands, as if trying to warm them. 'It was so awful. Seeing him there.'

'I know,' Hank said.

He had been getting out of his car when he heard her scream. He raced around the house, lashed by wind-blown leaves, dust stinging his eyes. A dozen terrible images bloomed in his mind in those few seconds it took him to reach her. He pictured her lying still, blood-soaked. He saw her falling, clutching at empty air. He cursed himself for leaving her alone. How could he have done it, no matter what he owed Charlie Carroll?

And then he saw her on her feet, her arms wide, and she was running towards him. He felt that he could breathe again. They raced to each other. He caught and held her. He felt her trembling. In that instant the long bad months when she had turned away from him were wiped away as if they'd never existed.

'Oh, Hank, thank God you're here!' she cried. 'It's Jake. Jake's in the pool. You've got to help me. He's in the pool, Hank. I think he's dead.'

That was when Hank saw the limp bloated body.

'I couldn't believe it,' she was saying. 'I thought he was a log. You know . . . one that Carl put in for the winter. And then . . . then . . . Oh, Hank, we've got to get him out!'

He released her. Standing at the pool's edge, he looked down. He knew death when he saw it. He'd learned to recognize it in Vietnam. After a moment, he said softly, 'We'd better not move him, Elianne.' Jake had been dead for days. That was obvious. Hank had seen such bloated bodies before.

He told her to go into the cottage, to dial 911 and ask for help.

'But Hank . . .'

'It's too late,' he said, and gave her a small push. 'Make the call. Hurry.'

She remembered going into the cottage. The television set was playing. Her fingers shook as she dialled.

Gordon had come out of the bedroom, Mandy following him, to demand angrily why she was there.

It had passed through Elianne's mind that they had been in bed, perhaps making love. That's why the set had been on, why all the lights had been burning.

When she told Gordon what had happened, he cursed. Mandy gave a frightened little cry.

By the time she had returned to Hank's side, there were sirens in the street, their wails dying in long moans before Hannah's Gate. There were flashing red lights. An ambulance. Police cars. A tide of people surged in. Flashlights. Hooks. A stretcher. Uniformed police. Police in plain clothes. Paramedics. Out of the milling confusion came order. The flicker and fading of flashbulbs. Finally Jake's body was taken from the pool limp and dripping.

Out of the order came questions. Elianne answered as well as she could. Jake Babbitt had been a friend of hers. He had been living at Hannah's Gate for about six months. He had no enemies that she knew of. He didn't know how to swim. He didn't have a steady job. That was all she could say. That was all anybody could say. All the while she spoke to them she thought of Ella Em. Would they investigate Jake's background? Would they go back into the past from which he'd come?

Her glance went to Hank. It had seemed so right and natural to be in his arms again. Was that Ella Em who had needed him? Or was it Elianne?

She had heard the police talking to the others. Gordon described Jake as a religious nut, living off his past friendship with Elianne. David added that Jake used drugs. Pot. LSD. He suggested that they search his room. They did and found the backpack, and took it away with them. Carl Utah told them he'd heard the commotion in front of Hannah's Gate from his nearby room, and had come over to see what was going on. Jake, Carl said, wanted to open a florist's shop. He spoke of how Jake had changed recently, shaved his beard and cut his hair. He drew a Jake Babbitt who was turning into a different man. Beginning a new life. Carl had said it was terrible that Jake had to die before that new man was born.

Elianne listened while Carl told the police about his relationship to Elianne and Gordon and David. He explained that only Elianne had known about it. When they asked why he had wanted the secrecy he had said, 'It was a feeling I had. That something was wrong.' Then he told them about Keith's death. 'It seemed like an accident, everybody thought. But still . . . Anyway, there were other things too. Small, maybe unimportant, but maybe they meant something. Handymen are kind of invisible, you know? So I thought I'd see more that way.'

Now, after midnight, the house was still again.

Gordon and Mandy had gone back to the cottage. David had retreated to his upstairs bedroom. Carl had wandered off.

Hank put down his coffee cup, and looked at Elianne. Her face was scored with fatigue, her brown eyes over-large and shiny with held-back tears. Her fingers were clenched in her hair. He wanted to gather her into his arms, to warm her with his own warmth. Instead he said gently, 'I need to tell you, Elianne . . . no matter what you feel for me, I am the same. I love you. Don't answer me now. Just remember it.'

She gave him a brief pain-filled glance. 'I can't think now,' she whispered finally. 'Not now, Hank.'

'Did Jake Babbitt mean so much to you?' he asked, his voice gentle.

'No. Not any more. But maybe at one time he did.' She could go that far and no further.

'Never mind, Elianne,' he said. 'Tomorrow will be a hard day too. You'd better get some rest.'

'In a little while,' she said.

But long after he had left her, she remained

in the study, still clutching her coffee cup. She thought about Jake. What had he meant to her? Why hadn't she sent him away as soon as he'd come to Hannah's Gate? She had once believed that she loved him. She owed him kindness for the kindness he had given her. She knew she could never explain to Hank the life she had had with Jake. She must carry the burden of her guilt alone. Guilt for a past that couldn't be changed, could only be accepted and endured.

It had nothing to do with Hank. Only with Ella Em and Elianne. She remembered that she had once thought Ella Em was dead, then she had realized that Ella Em and Elianne were the same. There was no Ella Em, there never had been. It was her way of separating herself from the memories she wanted to disown. She had tried to pretend to herself that she had been a different person then. But she hadn't been. She had been Elianne all along. Elianne with hard-to-bear memories, but Elianne still.

Now she had to consider the present. Daybreak came, the dark of the sky faded. A ray of pale sun crawled across the rug, rising higher until it reached the bookcase, glinting on the dictionary that had been her mother's.

Anna Taylor's words came back to Elianne. Terrible things had happened at Hannah's Gate when her mother was young. Two girls had been murdered. Somehow the family had survived. Now death had come here again. Keith had died. Had it been the accident they had supposed? Could she be sure of that? And what of the strange things that had happened to her? Did they have anything to do with Keith's death? Now Jake was dead too. What had happened to him? How had he died?

As she went upstairs to her room, listening to the thick cold silence of the house, she asked herself what would happen next.

When Gordon and Mandy went back to the cottage, he told her to go to bed. He wanted to stay up for a while. He didn't tell her that he had arranged for David to meet him later. He knew he should have done that before. When he heard about Elianne's Hallowe'en adventure, he'd thought about taking David out for dinner. Then Mandy had started nagging at him, and Gordon forgot about it. Now he had to talk to David. He wasn't sure of what he was going to say. He didn't plan to ask David any questions. He hadn't before. He didn't see any reason to ask them now. But he *did* want to talk to him. He hadn't worked out what he was going to tell David. Or how he would go about it. But he knew that something would come to him. It always had before.

When, finally, David met him at pool side, he said quietly, 'Hang around a minute, and I'll grab us a couple of beers.'

He returned to find David sitting near the woodpile, eyes fixed on the wistaria that partly covered Elianne's window.

Gordon sat down, handed him a beer. 'Are you okay?'

'Sure,' David said. 'What do you want? It's cold out here.'

'I've been thinking,' Gordon said softly. 'We have to decide what to do.'

Mandy, who stood at the cottage window, straining to listen to the whispers, nodded her head. She too had been doing some thinking. She left the window, and went to the big wardrobe in the bedroom. She studied the dresses hanging there, the suits and coats. Rows of shoes stood on the shelf above. She began very quickly to separate the new from the old.

Outside David asked. 'What do you mean, we've got to decide what to do? About what? Why?'

'Jake's death, David. It changes everything.'

'I guess it does. But so what?'

'I'll tell you so what. Hank's going to talk Elianne into getting married right away.'

'What makes you think so?'

'I'm certain, David.'

'They haven't been getting together any

more. I've been watching. I know.'

'You can't watch every minute.'

'It's not the same between them.'

'That's where you're wrong,' his brother said. 'They've fooled you, I guess.' Gordon breathed deeply. 'You'll see. With Jake dead, Hank's going to persuade her to marry him. If nothing else, he'll scare her into it. And then we're going to be in deep trouble.' He paused. 'In fact, I think the best thing for you is maybe to go away. Go off to college. That'll satisfy Elianne.'

'You mean it'll satisfy you,' David said sourly. 'That's all you want. To get rid of me.'

'David . . . what's wrong with you? Can't you see I'm just worried about you.'

'I can take care of myself.'

'Think about it,' Gordon said gently. 'I mean it. Think about getting away, David. While you can.'

Slowly David turned his head. He looked deep into Gordon's eyes.

Gordon steadily returned his gaze for a long moment. Then he got to his feet and went inside.

Mandy heard him at the cottage door and quickly shut the wardrobe. She'd done what she could. She could do some more tomorrow. A little at a time. One step before the next.

And then, when the day came, she'd be ready.

She turned, smiling, as Gordon came into the room. She went to him, arms wide, lips puckered for a kiss. 'Need some loving, baby?' she asked. 'It's been a bad day, hasn't it?'

David, meanwhile, went around the side of the house, and into Honey Locust Lane. Hands in his pockets, his head down, he walked for hours through the dark city streets.

He didn't want to go away from Hannah's Gate.

He wasn't going to go away from Hannah's Gate.

No matter what happened, he wasn't going to leave.

It was home, his and Gordon's. And no matter what Gordon said or did, David intended to stay there and claim it, and keep it for both of them.

The next morning the Washington *Post* Metro section carried a brief report of the suspicious death of a man named Jake Babbitt in Cleveland Park, and listed the address of the house at which it had occurred.

Carrie Day read it, and recognized the number and street. Hannah's Gate. So it was beginning again, she thought. Jake Babbitt . . . She'd never heard of him, but that didn't matter. She could get some mileage out of it anyhow. But she paused as she reached for the phone. What was the use? Her contacts were all gone. Some had retired. Some died. The youngsters running things nowadays didn't know or care about Hannah's Gate. No more than they knew or cared about Big Jack Gowan and his illegitimate daughter.

Carrie relaxed into the sofa again. She was surprised to realize that she didn't care any more either.

Elianne read the same article. It didn't matter. The reported words were nothing compared to the reality of what had happened. Keith was dead. Now Jake was dead too.

Because of her. Because she had come home to Hannah's Gate. She shivered. How would it end?

Detective Bill Eagan and his partner came back at noon. They shook raindrops from their hats, shrugged out of their damp overcoats and settled down with Elianne to ask more questions.

She told them what she had told them before. She had no idea of what could have happened to Jake. She knew none of his friends, if he had any here in Washington. He had changed in the past weeks; she didn't know why.

Detective Eagan told her that Jake Babbitt had been a false name, but he had been identified through his fingerprints. The FBI had a file on him dating back to the sixties. He'd taken part in the civil rights movement, and had once been arrested in a demonstration in Alabama. His name was Martin Dyer. His parents, living in Michigan, had been located. When the medical examiner released his body, it would be sent to them for burial.

Elianne listened, numb with shock. She'd had no idea that Jake Babbitt was a false name. She couldn't think of Jake as Martin Dyer.

The detective went on to tell her that the medical examiner's report would be issued later that day, but that Eagan had had an informal report by telephone. Jake had been struck on the head with an unpolished wooden object, had been unconscious but alive when he was put into the pool. It couldn't have been an accident. Not unless he'd fallen forward and knocked himself out, and then stood up, raised the tarpaulin and finally staggered into the pool. That was deemed impossible by the medical examiner. He, Eagan, agreed. So Jake's death was certainly a homicide. Analysis of the inside of Jake's backpack indicated the presence of crumbs of marijuana, and on a small wad of tissue paper there had been the powdered residue of LSD. What did Elianne know about the drugs? the detective wondered.

She told him that she had been poisoned by the acid, but that Jake had denied giving it to her. She hadn't taken it on purpose, she said. It had been a terrifying experience. Only Jake had saved her from hurting herself while she was under the influence of the drug.

The detective said slowly, 'No matter what he said, he could have given it to you.'

'Why would he?' she cried.

'Maybe to be the big hero by saving you,' the detective answered. 'It's been known to happen. Man saves girl. She falls for him out of gratitude.'

'No. That's not possible in this case,' she said.

Eagan didn't answer her, but he and his partner exchanged glances. The partner said, 'We're checking him out. We'll see. He spent a lot of time in Georgetown, we hear. People there recognize him from a picture we've circulated. We want to find out if he bought or sold drugs.'

'I don't believe it,' she said. 'But he *did* seem to be upset lately. Maybe scared. And not much ever scared Jake.'

'I guess he had reason to be this time,' Eagan told her.

He asked about Mandy Sommers, about

Carl Utah, about Hank. She told him everything that she could. Then he asked about her brothers. 'David's just a boy,' she protested. 'And Gordon had nothing to do with Jake.'

Soon after, they left Elianne, and went to talk to the others. None had any information, it appeared.

The detective stopped in the study to tell her that he'd be in touch when he knew more. She almost asked about Keith's death. Did the detective know about that? Could there be a connection to what had happened to Jake? But she stopped herself. Everyone believed Keith had died by accident. Only she felt uneasy about it. It would do no good now to distract the police with what might be a false trail. She said nothing.

She didn't realize that Bill Eagan had already checked out the file on Keith's death, and had seen that it was listed as accidental. He'd considered asking for an exhumation order, and a second autopsy, but then dismissed the idea. Accidents can happen in homes where murders later occur. He had enough to worry about without looking for more.

From an upstairs window Hank watched the police drive away. He had called Amy Carroll and explained what had happened. He wasn't going to the agency office that day, or any other day, until the mystery of Jake's death was solved. He wanted to keep an eye on Elianne. He was sure she was in danger. Too many things had happened. He had never accepted Keith's death as accidental. Now Jake had been murdered. It seemed to him that some unseen evil was creeping closer and closer to Elianne. He wasn't going to let anything happen to her.

Chapter Seventeen

By the end of the week, it was as if nothing had happened. The family gathered for dinner. Mandy, dressed in bright blue, with a gold chain at her throat and dangling gold earrings, was as gay as usual. She flirted alternately with David, Gordon and Hank. Gordon ate hugely, contributing little to the conversation. David was silent and watchful as usual.

Elianne slowly looked around the table. Yes, she thought, it seemed as if nothing had happened at Hannah's Gate. Except that Carl had joined the rest of them for the meal. He'd asked permission to stay at the house for a few days, and, of course, she had agreed. So he was here now. He was a hard person to figure out, but she trusted him; although she didn't know why. When Gordon and David had learned of his relationship to them, they'd hardly reacted. So he was an uncle of theirs, so what, was their attitude.

She glanced at the place where Jake had always sat. It was empty. Jake was gone. Keith had once had a seat at this table. It too was empty. He too was gone.

Hank sat across from her. Their eyes met. She couldn't tell what he was thinking. She looked hastily away.

She couldn't tell what her brothers were thinking either.

She wondered if they were asking themselves the same questions she was asking herself. What had happened to Jake? Maybe Keith too? Would the police ever find out?

After the meal was over, Hank came into the study where she was trying to read. For a little while, they spoke of inconsequential things: a new restaurant on Connecticut Avenue, the weather. But when he left her, she felt comforted. Maybe everything would be all right. Maybe this terrible sense she had of something coming was only in her imagination. Maybe Detective Eagan's theory was right: that Jake had been selling drugs and someone had come to Hannah's Gate to buy from him, and then killed him. She stilled the doubt that whispered a denial. Jake hadn't been selling drugs, no matter how she wanted to believe that.

When she went up to bed, a familiar stillness enclosed the house. She lay sleepless for several hours. The comfort of Hank's presence was gone now. Her fears returned to lie upon her with rock-like weight. David. Gordon. Could either one of them be responsible for what had happened? No. They were her brothers. They shared the same blood, shared the same lives. She wouldn't allow herself to remember them as children: heads together, Gordon whispering, David giggling. *Now* had nothing to do with *then*. She considered Mandy. But she couldn't have struck the blow that killed Jake. She wasn't strong enough, was she? And why would she have wanted to anyway? What of Hank? Oh, no, no. She couldn't doubt Hank. Not for an instant could she doubt him. And Carl? But she trusted Carl, even thought she knew so little about him. Not Carl. Then who was guilty? Finally she drifted off, her fears following her into sleep.

Gordon was watching television when Mandy came out of the bedroom. She was wearing her fur coat, the one he had bought her. She carried two Vuitton suitcases. He'd bought her those as well.

He stared at her. 'What the hell are you doing?'

'I'm bailing out, Gordie.'

'You're what?'

'I'm leaving,' she said. 'And don't try to stop me.'

'Mandy! You can't!'

She went to the door. 'Just watch,' she said, and smiled and blew him a kiss. 'Goodbye, Gordie.'

The door closed behind her. There was the tap of her heels on the paving. Soon the El Dorado started up. He heard it pull out. He imagined its tail lights gleaming in the dark. Within moments the sound of it was gone.

He was alone. He got up and went into the bedroom. He could still smell her perfume. Tangy, and very expensive. There were still clothes in the wardrobe. He supposed she'd left behind what she didn't want. He turned away.

He went back to sit before the television set, but he didn't hear the voices, nor see the moving figures. What was on the screen was a smeared and coloured blur that spit empty sounds at him. Mandy was gone. Now he would have nothing. No Mandy. No Hannah's Gate.

Hours later he decided that he had to talk to David. That was the only way. He went outside in his shirtsleeves and started through the cold night to the house.

The dream was one that Elianne had had before. Even in her sleep she recognized it. There was the sound of the wistaria scraping at the window, and an icy wind blowing across her face. A tall dark shadow stepped through the curtains and dropped silently to the floor. It drifted across the room to stand by her bed.

A faint rustle splintered the stillness. Warm breath grazed her cheek. Suddenly she was awake, torn from sleep. Heart pounding, she reared up, fighting the heavy quilt that lay on her. A scream built up and died in her throat.

Too late she knew it wasn't the familiar dream. *It wasn't a dream at all.* A cold hard hand lay across her mouth. Fingers clenched into her shoulder, pinning her down. No dream. No dream. She looked into David's glittering hazel eyes, his thin twisted face. David!

'You can't have Hannah's Gate,' he whispered in a deadly voice. 'It's Gordon's and mine. That's what Daddy wanted. He hated you, Elianne, because you came first. And he wanted Gordon to be first. His son. Then me. You couldn't get him to love you, no matter how you tried. Don't you remember how it was? How he hated you? Because he wanted Gordon and me to have Hannah's Gate. And that's how it's going to be.'

She remembered how it had been. Remembered trying to win love from a man who didn't have it to give. Her father. Jake. The other men she'd been with. Remembering, she struggled, but it was useless. She couldn't free herself from David's grasp. She tried to scream, but couldn't make a sound. His wiry strength, his madness, overwhelmed her.

He went on, 'Keith saw me spying on you and Hank, and understood what I was going to do. He warned me. He warned *me*, Elianne. So I showed him. Remember last spring at Skyline Drive? You nearly died then. A pity you didn't. Keith would still be alive if you had. And I liked Keith. Jake too. I *did* like him, but he figured out about the LSD. Too bad for Jake. But never mind. Now's as good a time as any, isn't it?' A smile twisted David's face then. 'You're wondering why I'm telling you. Not because confession's good for the soul. Only because I want you to know everything before you die.' Again he smiled. 'I want you to know what's going to happen, too.' Feeling her gather herself for one last try, he pressed harder on her mouth and shoulder. Her teeth cut into the inside of her lips, and she tasted blood. Sharp pain exploded in her shoulder. He said quietly, 'I'm going to suffocate you just until you pass out. And then, when you can't fight me, I'm going to drop you down Keith's lift shaft. You'll have a sad accident. Just one more of several that have happened at Hannah's Gate. And Gordon and I will live here forever after.'

She heaved against him. She kicked and writhed, but his hand held her mouth, his other hand thrust at her shoulder, and now his body lay across her hips. Desperation fuelling her struggles, she fought him. Slowly her face became wet with tears that spilled down her cheeks and around his hand. For an instant, her mouth slipped from beneath his dampened fingers.

She tried to scream, but only a quiet croak escaped her before he had her lips covered again, gagged by his hand. She was aware that there was a brief instant when he released her shoulder. She tried to fight him, but it was too late. She was weakening now. A pillow came down on her face. Blackness. No breath. She cried out, 'Hank!' But the plea for help was only in her mind. She was sinking, sinking. There was a roaring in her ears. A roaring, the pounding of blood.

Suddenly that terrifying sound was altered.

There were voices. Shouts. The bed shook beneath her. She was free. The pillow fell away from her face. She opened her eyes to find the room ablaze with light.

Hank came across the room in a headlong rush. His body bowled David over. They both went down in a tangle of thrashing arms and legs.

But David broke away. He was on his feet. He made for the window. Elianne clung to his legs as he tried to scramble up to the sill. Entangled with the curtains, he fell away from the window. He kicked her aside, and threw himself at the door.

Just beyond it Carl grabbed for him. David fought himself free. At that moment Gordon came into view at the top of the stairway.

'Come on, David! Run! Run!' Gordon cried. 'Get away, David!' He moved aside, out of the way, standing before the lift door.

David heard him, swerved deliberately, and crashed into him. Gordon thought that he was the one pulling the strings that moved David, but Gordon fooled himself. David listened to Gordon, but had his own plans. After Elianne, it would have been Mandy's turn. Then it would have been only David and Gordon. If they couldn't be together at Hannah's Gate one way, they would be another.

When David crashed into him, Gordon screamed. He fell backward, and his heavy body broke through the door, and crashed down to land on the top of the cage a floor below.

David hardly paused. With Carl reaching for him, and Hank coming at him, he leaped the steps, and disappeared into the dark of the lower hall.

His running footsteps echoed along the hallway. For a moment, there was a pause, then a loud crash. Finally a door slammed.

By that time, Carl was already climbing down the lift shaft to get to Gordon.

Hank was running downstairs, with Elianne at his heels. Her breath rasped in her throat. Her heart shuddered within her chest. David! David! Her own brother had tried to kill her. He'd slammed into Gordon, and run away. Where was he going? How did he hope to escape?

The hall chandelier burst into light as she reached the bottom of the stairs. She heard Hank thud into the kitchen and when she caught up with him, he was wrestling with a huge cupboard that blocked the door. When he saw that he couldn't move it, he climbed over it. It took what seemed a long time for him to get the kitchen door open. At last he did, and disappeared outside. Elianne was slower at climbing over the obstruction David had left behind. Finally, though, she managed it. Within moments then, she caught up with Hank.

He was standing still, staring up at the wistaria. He said softly, 'Don't look, Elianne.'

But it was too late. She had already seen the

313

long dark shape hanging from the bare limb. Hanging. Swaying. From above it, came the sharp nervous chittering of the disturbed squirrels.

Chapter Eighteen

The portrait of Big Jack Gowan was touched with the light of dawn when Elianne finished telling Detective Eagan and his partner about the dream that had been no dream. Then Hank and Carl explained that they'd both been concerned for Elianne's safety after Jake's death, and had agreed to watch over her. They'd heard a faint sound from her room, and had broken into it, but David had been able to elude them. They didn't know why Gordon had come up to the house at that time, nor why David had deliberately crashed into him before running away.

'Well, we do know enough,' the detective said finally shutting the notebook in which he had been writing. 'I guess we can mark these cases closed.'

In a little while, he and his partner rose to go. Hank and Carl went with them.

Elianne looked slowly around the study. Her great-grandfather's portrait. His old books on the shelves. Her mother's dictionary still on the table where she had always kept it. It was for this room, for Hannah's Gate, that David had tried to murder her. Poor David, always the puppet. And Gordon always pulling the strings. A club of two at the end as at the beginning. Two, against her. She remembered that there had been moments when she had blamed the house, blamed Hannah's Gate, for all the ills that had befallen those that lived there. Back in her mother's time, and now in her own. But the house was only wood and brick and mortar. What had happened had come from the nature of the people who lived there. The seeds of their fate had been in themselves. But Keith and Jake had been innocent victims. They had died because they'd tried to protect her. That much was plain from what David had said.

He had said something else too. The words gained resonance in her mind now. *Daddy hated you. No matter how you tried, he hated you.* She'd tried to win love from her father, from Jake, from the others she'd been with. When she failed, she learned to be afraid. To fear and distrust love. That's why she'd been so frightened when Hank spoke of marriage. She was afraid of love's vulnerability. But her doubts about Hank were gone. They had faded long before. She'd realized that when he pulled her away from David. She had nothing to fear from Hank. There had never been an Ella Em to be ashamed of. There had only been Elianne, confused and lost. But that was behind her. Not gone, for the past never dies. It reaches forward into the present. Not gone, but accepted, and with no power to hurt her any longer. From that past came this present. From this present would come the future. Her future. With Hank.

He came to the door of the study, hesitated on the threshold.

She rose, smiling, and opened her arms to him.

Hannah's Gate still stands in Cleveland Park. It looks much the same as it did when Carl Utah gave Elianne away the day she married Hank. The honey locust trees foam with white blossoms in the spring, and the air is filled with the lemony scent of fresh magnolias. Generations of squirrels continue to nest in the spreading wistaria vine. But now three children play in the shadow of the red brick walls, and the old house echoes to their laughter.

We hope you have enjoyed this Large Print book. Other Thorndike Press or Chivers Press Large Print books are available at your library or directly from the publishers. For more information about current and up-coming titles, please call or write, without obligation, to:

Thorndike Press
P.O. Box 159
Thorndike, Maine 04986
USA
Tel. (800) 223-6121 (U.S. & Canada)
In Maine call collect: (207) 948-2962

OR

Chivers Press Limited
Windsor Bridge Road
Bath BA2 3AX
England
Tel. (0225) 335336

All our Large Print titles are designed for easy reading, and all our books are made to last.